Praise for *I Learned a New Word Today...Genocide*

"This is a lovely and moving book. As someone who teaches genocide at a university level, I've often wondered how I would grapple with the challenge of conveying the subject to a younger audience – both the horror of the events, and the opportunities for intervention and positive social change. Elizabeth Hankins has accomplished that task superbly. Her humane and accessible tale will captivate not only younger readers, but many of their elders as well."

Adam Jones, Ph.D., author of *Genocide: A Comprehensive Introduction*

"Elizabeth has the ability to discuss some of the hardest issues facing humanity in a way that leaves the reader with hope rather than frustration about the evil in this world. Genocide continues to scar the lives of countless innocent people, and "the only thing necessary for evil to triumph is", as Edmond Burke stated, "for good men to do nothing." It has never been more critical for us to instill in the hearts and minds of our children a deep commitment to guard the sanctity of human life, and I believe Elizabeth's vital work will help to do exactly that. She has written about the reality of genocide in a way children can understand, using her strong sense of conviction that we are our brother's keeper and that each of us can use our voice to stand for truth and justice, and inspire future leaders to live for the noble cause of protecting the innocent."

U.S. Congressman Trent Franks, Arizona

"*I Learned a New Word Today...Genocide* is an example of the powerful way to educate our youth to become changemakers. The historical references to 20th century genocides, and the complex web of politics that surround the issue, are presented in a way that will help children understand that they too can play a role in the prevention of genocide and mass atrocities."

Sam Bell, executive director of Genocide Intervention Network

"Principled without being preachy and serious but not too solemn, this book is exactly what young people need to read to understand one of the darkest parts of human history. The good news is that we can prevent genocide from happening, but it requires a sober understanding of what has taken place and a call to action so that history does not repeat itself. With this book, Elizabeth Hankins gives a gift to everyone who knows and loves a young person. Buy it and pass the gift on to another. You and they will be richer for it!"

D. Michael Lindsay, Ph.D., author of *Faith in the Halls of Power*

"*I Learned a New Word Today...Genocide* capitalizes upon the unique opportunity to breed a generation of political will and conscience through education. Children who learn about the atrocities of the twentieth century today will evolve into the constituency that continues to stand up against human rights abuses in Darfur, Burma, and Congo, now and in the future. Hankins demonstrates to her young readers that with time and dedication, their collective outcry will move the international community to action."

Emily Cunningham, Massachusetts state coordinator, and Greg Kuo, director of Teach Against Genocide

"*I Learned a New Word Today...Genocide* is a powerful book that will educate children about genocide, teaching them indelible lessons about defending the powerless and protecting life. This essential book will shape young lives and install a lifelong commitment to end genocide and mass atrocities once and for all!"

Cory Smith, human rights attorney and faith outreach advisor

"For years now, I've lived with and moved among victims of genocide. For many of us, genocide is a foreign term with generic statistics, too overwhelming and distant to process. In reality, genocide is intensely personal – it's faces, it's names, it is our brothers and sisters. *I Learned a New Word Today...Genocide* personalizes genocide for all of us. It is skillfully crafted, a captivating read for the reader of any age. Yet even more, it compels one to action. I treasure this book and wholeheartedly endorse it. May we all be powerfully moved."

Peter Swann, executive director of Aid Sudan

"Out of a heart of compassion for the world, author Elizabeth Hankins has a birthed *I Learned a New Word Today...Genocide*. And out of a faith in the compassion of young people the world over, and a faith in their desire to do justice and love mercy, she has given the responsibility of telling this story of the sobering reality of genocide to a fifth grader, Javier Mendoza. I urge you to read Hankins' book, and, with hope and love, to give it to the young people you know who will be the world-changers we so desperately need."

Faith J. H. McDonnell, director, Religious Liberty Program and Church Alliance for a New Sudan, The Institute on Religion and Democracy, Washington, DC; author of *Girl Soldier: A Story of Hope for Northern Uganda's Children*.

I LEARNED A NEW WORD TODAY...
GENOCIDE

ELIZABETH HANKINS

KPH

First Edition 2009
The Key Publishing House Inc.
Toronto, Canada
Website: www.thekeypublish.com
E-mail: info@thekeypublish.com

ISBN 978-0-9811606-0-3

Cover design: Olga Lagounova
Proofreading: Jennifer South
Typesetting and image design: Velin Samarov

Cover design is inspired by a Thomas Campbell photograph (www.thomasgcampbell.com).

Library and Archives Canada Cataloguing in Publication

Hankins, Elizabeth,
    I Learned a New Word Today...Genocide/ Elizabeth Hankins.

ISBN 978-0-9811606-0-3

    1. Genocide–Juvenile fiction. I. Title.
PS3608.A557I2 2009   j813'.6   C2009-902641-4

Printed and bound in USA. This book is printed on paper suitable for recycling and made from fully sustained forest sources.

Published in association with, and a grant from The Key Research Centre (www.thekeyresearch.org). The Key promotes freedom of thought and expression and peaceful coexistence among the people of the world. Our publications aim to bring tolerance, respect, mutual understanding, peace, harmony and happiness to our human society.

FOR MADDIE HANKINS AND MAX BROWN. YOU HAVE SOULS LIKE THE GIANTS WHO HAVE RE-WRITTEN HISTORY. AND FOR BEN AND KINSEY BROWN, JORDAN AND LUKE PERKINS AND JILLIAN SMITH. YOUR BRILLIANT MINDS AND GREAT HEARTS ARE REMINDERS THAT ANYTHING IS POSSIBLE...

FOREWORD

"What seems to us more important, more painful, and more unendurable is really not what is more important, more painful and more unendurable, but merely that which is closer to home. Everything distant which for all its moans and muffled cries, its ruined lives and millions of victims, that does not threaten to come rolling up to our threshold today, we consider endurable and of tolerable dimensions."

— Aleksandr Solzhenitsyn

Through the journal of eleven-year-old Javier Mendoza, Elizabeth Hankins brings the horrors of past and ongoing genocides closer to our threshold. And without a doubt, we cannot consider any of them endurable.

The twentieth century was the bloodiest century in the history of mankind. More than 100 million persons were killed in our wars; another 100 million persons were deprived of living happy, fruitful, and contributing lives because of political repression, systematic killing of "the other" - genocide.

So then, are wars and genocide inevitable? To this, I would offer a resounding "no" though I recognize that many believe violent conflict is the natural state of man, an unavoidable malady. And to the argument that the best we can hope for is minimizing "collateral damage" as nations and peoples war to win – and then hold fast to power by every means imaginable in hopes of remaining victorious when the next conflict arises – I would offer an alternative vision to consider.

To be sure, history *does* seem to support the inescapable cycle of violence argument. Yet I believe, as Elizabeth Hankins does, that sustainable peace must be worked for – and *can* be achieved. What I mean by "sustainable peace" is a diverse community striving together, across all that usually divides us, to meet the needs of all of its members.

And who builds such a community?

Imagine living in a society where a critical mass of people decide over and again, in countless small decisions everyday, to seek the interests of others – the common good – and not just the good of themselves. Then imagine these same individuals working tirelessly to influence the structures of their society – the organizations, companies, governments – to do the same.

Oscar Romero wrote: "Peace is not the product of terror or fear. Peace is not the silence of cemeteries. Peace is not the silent result of violent repression. Peace is the generous, tranquil contribution of all to the good of all. Peace is dynamism. Peace is generosity. It is right and it is duty."

So then forging that kinder, more generous critical mass may be more of a reality than we imagine. And perhaps our journey toward it begins when we commit to bear witness not only to that which is broken and horrific in our world, but the truth that each one of us can – and should – make a difference. We see this principle reflected simply, yet eloquently, in *I Learned a New Word Today...Genocide.*

I hope that teachers of young readers nationwide will give this book to their students to help them understand how our world works and what will be required of them to change history and build a different future. I hope that children will read and shudder with Javier. Yet I hope they'll not just be saddened, but instead choose to commit, as he does "to do that thing they can do to make a difference."

And I hope that many, many adults will do the same.

Randall Butler
The Institute for Sustainable Peace

PREFACE

I was in Washington, D.C. with about forty-five minutes between meetings when I remembered a promise I'd made. I hailed a taxi, jumped in and headed to the National Archives in search of a national treasure.

Just the week before, my ten-year-old daughter's close friend stood in our kitchen examining the Declaration of Independence that we keep on our refrigerator. While I got dinner together, we talked about this great document, about the spirit behind it, the striving that had come with it. We talked about the ordinary men with extraordinary resolve who had done the things that they could do to relieve oppression and tyranny. In the process, they had formed a new nation and helped rewrite history.

Before she went home, my daughter's friend told me that she would like her own copy of the Declaration and I told her the next time that I went to D.C., I would gladly oblige.

At the Archives, the lines were scant, the gift shop nearly empty—so within minutes, I'd taken care of business and was back out on Pennsylvania Avenue. The September morning was clear, the sun already high in the sky, with a light breeze blowing. I plunked down my backpack, unzipped it and slipped the Declaration inside.

That's when I got the idea.

A young adult book about genocide. A book for older kids (between fifth and ninth grade) that unpacks the complicated nature of genocide in a way that not only educates, but helps inspire action.

It made sense to me. Kids care. They just do. They care about stuff that we adults often forget we're supposed to care about.

They care about scrawny kittens with missing tails and birds with broken wings. They dig deep into their pockets when they see a homeless guy asking for money and when they hear stories of human suffering anywhere, their first compulsion is usually compassion.

So telling the story of genocide through the eyes of an eleven-year-old immigrant learning about it for the first time seemed like a good idea to me. It seemed good for two reasons: One, older children can grasp the constructs of genocide the same way they can follow the events that led up to the fall of Rome or the rise to globalism. They can—and should—understand the world around them and how this world works. The second reason I think that a novel like this works is it educates to inspire change. *I Learned a New Word Today...Genocide* isn't just a book highlighting instances of man's gravest inhumanities to man. To the contrary, it's a story that brings its young readers to crossroads of their own: When faced with oppression, will they choose compassion? When tyranny is present, will they rise and stand for the freedom and protection of the defenseless?

Like Javier Mendoza, will they find the thing that they can do—and then do it?

I believe in our world's very young people. I believe that when presented with age-appropriate information about even the most difficult issues, they comprehend, care and want to take actions of their own. And when they're given these opportunities to catalyze change, something else happens.

They change, too. There's something life-altering about seeking justice and peace for those who cannot secure it for themselves.

Something else: Kids who care usually grow up and become adults who care. They become the next generation of culture makers—of politicians and activists, of teachers and doctors and clergy and so on. And if along the path of their becoming they've learned to overturn injustice with action, indifference with fortitude, then perhaps making genocide history is more of a reality than we imagine.

CHAPTER 1

DEAR JOURNAL:

I learned a new word today. It was a word I had never heard. And I did not like the sound of it.

In a minute I will tell you the word, but first I should probably tell you more about me. Then I will tell you what I learned today. And I will tell you what I will be studying for the next six weeks in my social studies class.

Mr. Steinberg (who is my social studies teacher) says we all need to write down what we learn. We also need to write the thoughts that we think about the stuff that we are studying. He said that we should write as much as we can, and I think that this is a good idea because besides playing on my Wii™, my favorite thing to do is read and write things down.

So I guess I will do what my teacher says. And even though a journal is not a person who needs to know about you, I think it is a good thing to tell you some things about me before all of this writing gets started.

My name is Javier Mendoza and I am almost eleven years old. I am in the fifth grade and I have two sisters. I had a brother, but he died in the war in Iraq. He was a soldier and I miss him.

My sisters are kind of old. Carmen is fifteen and Liliana is twenty-one. They both live with me, our dog Hombre and my father in our apartment. We live in Washington, D.C., which is the capital of the United States. My father, Pedro, is a facilities manager for one of the biggest buildings in Washington. This means that his job is to make sure that all of the rooms in his big building get taken care of. He says that this is hard work and I believe him because every night he comes home very tired. He is quiet while we eat the dinner that I help Liliana make if I am in a helpful mood. Then he checks my homework and reminds me and my sisters how important education is. He tells us that we must study very hard.

Liliana always agrees with Papa and I think that this is because she is studying very hard at Georgetown University. Georgetown is a good university here in Washington, D.C., and the people who go to school there spend a lot of their time in little groups. In these groups, they drink Pepsi, eat candy and pizza and talk about things like taking tests. They ask each other a million questions about notes and what they will do during the weekend if they do not have to go to work or be in another little group to study for more tests.

Sometimes the groups come to our apartment to eat and talk and look at their books with Liliana. While they do this, I listen to their conversations while I play on my Wii™. I try to be so nicely behaved that some girl student will think that I am a good little brother. When this happens, I always get a piece of their pizza and sometimes even a candy bar.

My father is from Mexico and my mother is from Colombia. I do not see my mother very much. This is because she stays in Mexico to take care of Papa's mama, who is very old now.

I go to school at Franklin D. Roosevelt Elementary in downtown Washington, D.C. My school was named after America's thirty-first president and there is a huge picture of him and his wife, Lady Eleanor, just outside of the school office. President Roosevelt is not smiling in this picture and sometimes I think that he looks like our principal, Mr. Franklin Tate. Except Mr. Tate is a little bit younger and he can smile when he wants to.

So now I will tell you some more about my social studies unit that is coming — and the word that we learned today.

Genocide.

That's the word we learned.

It means destroying a certain group of people. Sometimes even a whole group of people.

I did not like the sound of that.

Mr. Steinberg says that we need to learn about genocide because it is part of our history. He says it is part of our history as human beings, even though it is very sad and tragic history. But he says that if we learn about genocide when we are young, we will understand it better. We will be aware that genocide does not suddenly just start one day. It is something that happens when certain things go wrong in different places of the world. And when these things go wrong, there are not people or groups that are around to help make it right again.

That's when very bad things start to happen. But Mr. Steinberg says that if students like the fifth graders at Roosevelt Elementary begin to understand things about genocide, they might start to care about how they can help. And my teacher said that when people care about stuff together, the world can become different.

I do not know what I think about this but it sounds like a good idea. Maybe if more people cared and helped, there would not be any more genocides. So those very bad things that happen during genocides would stop.

I hope this can happen.

Anyway, tomorrow we will go to the United States Holocaust Memorial Museum. This museum is just a few minutes from my school, but Mr. Steinberg says that we have to take the bus because keeping up with twenty-five boys and girls is like trying to keep kittens in a box.

I like kittens a lot, especially little black ones with blue eyes. But they are hard to keep up with. Besides, it is pretty cold outside and Mr. Steinberg said that walking there might be easy.

But after we see some of the stuff in that museum, the walk back to school might not be.

CHAPTER 2

HI JOURNAL,

I am only writing tonight because Mr. Steinberg said that we have to write something about what we saw today. He said we are all getting grades on our journals and that we should try to write something almost every day of the week except Saturdays and Sundays.

This is fine with me because mostly I like writing. Plus, he said we could take notes in class and then re-write them in our journals later on. Taking notes is good because I would probably forget about what I am supposed to learn and then only write about my plans for new adventures. I like adventure and I am very clever at making some good ones up.

I heard that word again today. And I am very serious when I say that I do not like it.

Genocide. It means doing and planning things that destroy a group of people. Sometimes even a whole group of people.

Besides just hearing that word, our class saw things at the Holocaust Museum that totally creeped me out. They creeped me out because the things that we saw are some of the very bad things that happen during a genocide.

After school, I wanted to talk to Liliana about these things because when I feel sad or afraid, she asks me to sit next to her and she does not ask me too many questions. She doesn't try to hug me or anything. She just stays quiet until I am ready to say something. While she waits, she usually twists her ponytail, which is really long and the color of the black ink that drips out of my pen when I chew on it and it accidentally leaks everywhere. And if I cry—which I almost never do since I am nearly eleven—she moves closer to me and puts her arm around me like Mama does.

But Liliana was still at school when I got home. Only Carmen was around. And I could tell she was not in a good mood because she was saying words in Spanish that sometimes get her into trouble with Papa. They were not really bad words, but they were the ones that Papa and Liliana say are full of attitude.

Carmen was in charge of making dinner tonight and I think that she was not happy about that. I was not happy either because whenever Carmen makes dinner, it means I have to eat canned beans with slimy hot dogs cut up into little pieces. Then I have to act like she has made something really good. If I don't, Papa gives me a look that means be grateful or go to your room.

So I just went into my room and closed the door (but not because I won't eat beans and slimy hot dogs later). I sat on the floor and dug my finger into the black spot on my carpet that is shaped like an elephant's footprint. Only the spot is not nearly as big. It came from one of my pens that leaked ink because I was chewing on it too hard.

I am going to tell you tomorrow what I saw today, Journal. I just do not want to do it now.

But I will tell you this: What I saw was terrible. It made my stomach hurt and my mind feel all fuzzy. Because when one person is hurt, or when one person dies, this is very sad.

But when millions of people get hurt or killed on purpose... well, this is so wrong and sad, I do not even know what to say.

CHAPTER 3

DEAR JOURNAL,

Today is Wednesday. I like Wednesdays because Papa comes home early and my friend Maker Jok comes over to my house to eat dinner. Maker's family is from Africa, from a country called Sudan. His father, Jengmer, and his mother, Achol, live with him in the same apartment complex as me and my family. We play together on Wednesday nights because both of his parents have to work on Wednesdays and there is no one to watch Maker. Except us.

Maker will come here in one hour, so I better hurry up and tell you what I saw yesterday. Otherwise I will not be able to play with him. Then I will be very sad because we always play chess, and since Maker plays chess better than me, I will not have a chance to make my game stronger.

So yesterday: We went to the United States Holocaust Memorial Museum. But before we went inside the big and serious-looking building, Mr. Steinberg told us that we would be studying some of the genocides that have happened in the past century. A *century* is one hundred years, in case you do not know. He said we would start by learning about the Holocaust.

I did not know what a holocaust was but I did not want to say so. I guess the other kids did not know either because Rachel Ling raised her hand and so did Luke Johnson. But Mr. Steinberg told them to put their hands down. He told them that he knew that his fifth grade class did not know what the Holocaust was. He said that was why we had come to this museum.

We would learn inside, Mr. Steinberg said. We would learn and see some of the things in this museum.

But what we saw would definitely surprise us. What we learned would be hard to believe. And we would see some things that might make us very sad.

But our teacher said that these things are part of our human history. And he said that if we do not remember some of the very bad things that should never happen, we might forget to do the right thing in the future.

Mr. Steinberg said that we would be witnesses when we got inside of the museum. He said that *witnesses* are people who see something for themselves—and then they tell other people what they saw.

I did not feel very much like a witness even though I am not sure what a witness is supposed to feel like. I just felt sort of hungry because Carmen made my breakfast this morning. I think Liliana needs to teach her to cook because she burned the beans and hot dogs last night. Then she put the leftovers in a tortilla for me to eat for breakfast. When no one was looking, I fed it to Hombre. He does not mind Carmen's food at all.

Okay, back to my story. So then we went inside that museum where a skinny girl with curly yellow hair and a big smile met us. I think that she was about the same age as Liliana and she told us her name was Kate. She told us that she liked fifth graders and that she would be helping us learn more about the Holocaust.

Next we went into a little room and Kate told us this true story:

A long time ago in the year 1933, a man called Adolph Hitler became the leader in Germany. Germany is not on our continent of North America. It is on the continent of Europe, which is pretty far away.

Anyway, Hitler had a group of people that followed him. They were loyal to him and did what he said to do. This group of German soldiers was called the Nazi Party. Hitler and his Nazi Party took charge of Germany in January 1933. Right away, they used their power to do terrible things to another group of people called the Jews.

Let me explain more about the Jews because Kate explained them to us. Jews are people who are Jewish. They are people with a history that traces back to the beginning of civilization. Originally, they lived in what is now the Middle East. Jewish people have certain beliefs about God and about ways to live their lives.

This is true about other religions and people, Kate explained to us. Christians and Buddhists and Muslims and other religions also believe certain things about God and about living a life of faith.

But Adolph Hitler did not like the Jewish people. He also did not like some other groups of people who were not German like him. He did not like the Roma people. The Roma were thought to have originally come from India. In some history books, the Roma people are also called the Gypsies.

Hitler also did not like people from Africa. He did not like people from Russia or from Poland, and he did not like people who believed differently than he did. He also did not like people who were handicapped or sick.

But most of all, Hitler did not like Jewish people.

He thought that the Jewish people had made Germany—and the countries that Germany worked with to fight the First World War—lose the war.

Hitler hated the Jewish people very much for this. He also hated that the Jewish people in Germany were very good at what they did. They were successful in their jobs, they worked hard and enjoyed living in Germany and helping serve their country.

But Hitler said that the Jews were inferior to the other Germans with light-colored hair and blue eyes. *Inferior* means less than—and Hitler thought that Jewish people and some of the other people like the Roma and Africans and others were much less important than the Germans. He thought that the Germans were a perfect race of people.

So Hitler made up a *conspiracy* (this means a sneaky master plan) to get rid of the people that he did not like.

But he concentrated most of his attention on hurting the Jewish people. And he started his plan very soon after he gained power in Germany.

Right away, Hitler and his Nazi Party began taking away the rights of the Jewish people. Pretty soon, Jews could not write about their own ideas. They could not say what they thought in public and they could not assemble (which means get together in groups) to talk about their opinions.

Then Hitler and his people made up laws that forbid Jewish people from owning property or having professional jobs like that of a doctor or lawyer or business person.

I thought that Kate would stop this story about the Jewish people after she told us all of this. I was tired of what she was saying and I did not like it. I looked across the room at Rachel Ling. I think that she wanted the story to be done, too, because she was biting her lip. That is what Rachel does when she is upset or worried. She bites her lip, sometimes until it bleeds. I know this because she sits in front of me in class. We sit in alphabetical order and her name begins with L; mine starts with M.

But Kate did not stop the story. She looked at Mr. Steinberg and Mr. Steinberg tugged on his beard and nodded his head.

Then Kate told us what happened next to the Jewish people.

The Nazis began to control everything in Germany and they made up untrue stories about the Jews. They told these stories on the radio. They told them in newspapers, in movies and in classrooms where students were learning. Kate explained that this was called *anti-Semitic propaganda*, which meant that a bunch of false information about the Jewish people was being told. The lies were meant to encourage other Germans to have anger and hate for the Jews.

In the summer of 1934, Adolph Hitler became the "absolute ruler" or *Fuhrer* in Germany. By September of the next year, there were laws (Kate said they were called the Nuremberg Laws of 1935—I remember this name because *Nurem* rhymes with Durham and Mr. Durham is my favorite sacker at the grocery store where Liliana gets our fruit; I remember the *berg* part because it reminds me of hamburgers and I love hamburgers) that said Jews were no longer citizens of Germany and that they could not marry anyone other than another Jewish person.

Now Anti-Semitism was part of the rules in Germany.

Jewish people were not citizens.

They had no rights and could not have property.

They could be—and were—mistreated. And it was their own government that was the main group hurting them!

Then came a really big night that changed everything. Actually, Kate said it was the night that marked the beginning of the Holocaust.

Before Kate could tell us some more about this night, Ahmed Naghavi raised his hand. This is something that Ahmed does not usually do because he is very smart and knows almost everything. But he asked Kate to tell us what *holocaust* meant.

Kate gave our whole class a sad little smile and she took a deep breath. Then she explained that in the dictionary, the word *holocaust* means a great devastation or destruction. It also could mean a sacrifice that is completely consumed by fire.

I think that we all must have looked confused because Kate hurried up and started telling us some more.

She told us that there was another definition of holocaust that we would learn about today. The Holocaust we would study in this big museum was an event that had happened. It was a terrible event that included the organized mass slaughter of more than six million Jewish people who lived in Europe during the Second World War. *Slaughter* means to be killed in a very brutal way. And Kate said that the Jews were killed violently by Hitler's Nazi Party and those people and groups that helped them. She said that we would see some of these ways today. Besides the Jews, millions more people were killed by the Nazis.

These huge numbers of killings in such a short period of time had never happened in history before.

Anyway, Kate said that the bad things that were happening to the Jewish people only got much, much worse. And the event that got the most terrible things started was called *Kristallnacht*. This is the German word that means the Night of Broken Glass.

Kristallnacht happened on November 9, 1938 when a Jewish teenager named Herschel Grynspan shot his gun at a German embassy official in Paris, France. Herschel was upset because of how the Jews were being treated. He was also angry for how his parents had been handled by the Nazis.

The official, who was named Ernst vom Rath, died from Herschel's gunshot. When he died, the Nazi Party used this as an excuse to carry out the first pogrom against the Jews. A *pogrom* is an organized plan to destroy or do terrible things to a group of people.

So the Nazis killed almost one hundred Jewish people in Germany that night. They stormed through areas where the Jewish people lived and broke windows in their houses. The Nazis destroyed thousands of Jewish shops and businesses and set fire to hundreds of synagogues. *Synagogues* are the places where Jewish people get together to worship God. Then they arrested around 30,000 Jewish men. The Nazis took these men to places called *concentration camps*.

Kate told us that she would let Mr. Steinberg explain more about concentration camps during our social studies classes. But she said that concentration camps were terrible places. They were not like summer camps or places where people just go to rest and think. She also said that after the Night of Broken Glass, the Holocaust had pretty much begun. Adolph Hitler and his Nazis were getting very serious about their plan to get rid of the Jewish people in Europe.

Hitler liked his power a lot and he wanted some more of it. In fact, he didn't just want to be in charge of Germany. He and his Nazi Party began conquering other countries in Europe. He started by taking over Austria in 1938. Then he invaded Poland and this started World War II. In 1940, he took over Denmark, Belgium, Holland, France, Norway and Luxembourg.

All of these countries had Jewish people living in them. But Poland had the most. There were more than three million Jews in Poland. And when Hitler defeated this country, he and his Nazis made sure that these Jewish people all got collected together. Then they were forced into very crowded ghettos (a *ghetto* is a not very nice section of a city where people who don't have much money often live) that had big walls around them. And they could not get out.

These ghettos were horrible places to live. There was hardly any food to eat and they were all crammed with people. Soon, tons of Jewish people starved to death or got diseases that killed them. All of the ghettos were awful and everyone suffered—but the largest one was the Warsaw Ghetto in Warsaw, Poland.

Kate told us that the man who eventually ordered the destruction of the Warsaw Ghetto was named Heinrich Himmler (but he only did this because he had even more horrible things in mind for the Jewish people). Himmler was in charge of getting the German police called the Gestapo and the Nazi SS to do unbelievable and terrible things to the Jews for Hitler. The Nazi SS (SS stands for *Schutzstaffel*, which is the German word for protective squad or guards) was made up of fierce young soldiers who believed in and did everything Hitler said he wanted done. They were very loyal to their Fuhrer—even when he was planning things that were incredibly evil.

Here is one more thing that I want you to know: Just because Hitler and his Nazi Party wanted to kill all of the Jews, this did not mean that all of the German people in Germany wanted to hurt Jewish people. This is also true of people in the other countries that Hitler kept taking over. There were many, many people who knew that Hitler's ways were cruel and very wrong. And a lot of them made a plan to hide the Jewish people and keep them safe from the Nazis.

Okay, Journal, I think I have said enough for now. My hand is tired from writing all this and Maker will be here in five minutes. But since I am supposed to write something about what I saw in that museum today, I will do it before I go to sleep. After Maker leaves. He promised to show me how to castle tonight and I really want to beat him in chess soon.

So later on I will tell you more.

✳ ✳ ✳

HI J (I THINK I WILL CALL YOU J BECAUSE JOURNAL IS TOO LONG),

I am back but this has gotta be real quick because I want to go to sleep.

After that big pogrom that Kate called the Night of Broken Glass, and as Adolph Hitler kept taking over other countries, things only got worse for the Jewish people. Pretty soon, that man, Himmler, who was very much in charge of carrying out Hitler's plans, ordered a place to be built that would keep the prisoners. The place was called Auschwitz. I still cannot say this word, and I can only write it because I copied it down when I got back to class and Mr. Steinberg wrote it on the board. But anyway, Auschwitz was made to hold Polish people who were Jewish. These Jews would be forced to go to Auschwitz, where they had to work very hard and not get paid any money for their work. This prison place was called a *concentration camp*. There would be many more of these places built. This is because as Hitler kept invading countries that had lots of Jewish people, he and his Nazis wanted to have a place to imprison all of them.

In the middle of 1941, which was sixty-seven years ago, Hitler and his Nazis did this really bold thing. I mean bold in a bad way, not a good way. They invaded the Soviet Union, which is now Russia, plus some other little countries close to it. But inside of the Soviet Union was about three million more Jewish people.

Now Hitler really wanted to get rid of the Jews. He wanted to get rid of all Jewish people in the countries where he was in charge.

So Kate said he ordered the "Final Solution" to the problem of there being so many Jewish people.

Hitler and his Nazis decided to kill all of the Jews so there would not be any more of them!

Let me tell you how this happened because I saw a lot of the ways these terrible things were done.

When we left the little room with Kate, and our class started following her and Mr. Steinberg through the big museum, we saw pictures from the Night of Broken Glass. We saw pictures of very scared-looking Jewish people. They were being forced into ghettos and back out of ghettos. We saw other pictures of Polish Jews wearing these yellow stars on their clothes. The Nazis made them wear these, but not to be nice or make the Jews feel special. They were used as a way of marking Jewish people as being different from other people that the Nazis liked.

Later, different colored patches got used to tell things about prisoners in the concentration camps. For instance, some people had to wear little black triangles. Kate said this was a symbol for the Roma and for other groups of people that were not acceptable to the Nazis.

We saw a picture of pretty ladies in dresses. They were holding the hands of their little children while Nazi soldiers were forcing them toward somewhere. We looked at pictures of men wearing baggy striped pants and shirts that looked like pajamas. We saw awful rusty railroad cars that Kate said had carried Jewish people to be prisoners in concentration camps and victims killed in extermination camps. There were six major extermination camps in Poland.

Then we saw a big room full of shoes. There were shoes of every shape and size and in so many styles that I could not count. Kate said that these were the shoes of the Jewish people who had died in the camps. When they got to these various camps, many of the Jews got shot by Nazis with guns. Many Jews got killed in special, horrible rooms called gas chambers.

And others had to take off their clothes and put on the blue striped clothes that looked like pajamas. The people in these striped clothes were not killed right away. They were the ones who had to work in the camps. While they did this, they were treated terribly. Eventually they got so tired and sick and starving that they died. Many of the Jewish women and girls in the camps had all of their hair shaved off. The hair was sent back to Germany and sold for money. At other camps, the Jewish prisoners were forced to have numbers tattooed on their left arms.

More than six million Jewish people died before World War II ended in 1945. Millions died because the Nazis killed them in these death camps and some Jews were starved to death in the ghettos. Others were worked or shot to death (I think close to two million were shot). Before they died, the Nazis often did horrible things to the bodies of the Jewish prisoners. And besides killing about two thirds of the Jewish people in Europe, these Nazis killed millions of other people. Some of these were the Gypsies (Roma people), handicapped people and also Russian people, black German people, Polish people and more.

Mr. Steinberg said this was called a genocide. The Holocaust was an enormous genocide.

I thought a lot about what Kate said and about what I saw at the museum. I thought about the millions of people who got killed by other people. And I thought about that word Mr. Steinberg uses for it all.

I wanted to tell Maker about that word because I think he comes from a country where a lot of people have been killed by a brutal government like Adolph Hitler's. I know about this because I heard Liliana talking about Maker and his family to some people in one of her little groups.

But my head felt too fuzzy about all of this to tell Maker. And by the time he had taught me to castle and I finally won a game of chess, it was time for him to go home. And actually, I was glad that he needed to go. Not because I wanted him to leave. Maker is one of my best friends, even if he is only in fourth grade.

I just did not want to explain that word. And I really did not want to think about what I saw yesterday.

CHAPTER 4

HI J,

Today is a good day! Papa just told us all at dinner that Mama is coming here for Christmas. This means that I get to see her in about six weeks and some days!

I miss Mama a lot. But I pretend that I do not because I will be eleven next week and Papa says that I am a man of the house, too. Mostly I do not feel like a man, though. This is because I am short with a round belly and black hair that sticks up like hundreds of antennae on my head. I have big ears and my nose runs every fall and spring, and all of this makes me think that I am not very much like a man.

Anyway, I usually pretend to be very strong like Papa. And Papa does not say anything about missing Mama even though I know that he does.

But now she will come home and spend three months with us because Papa's sister, my Aunt Rosalita, will come to take care of Abuela. *Abuela* means grandmother in Spanish and it is the name that I call my Papa's mama.

When she comes, I will tell Mama about genocide even though talking about it makes me feel like I am walking on one of those rickety bridges that bounce and rock back and forth until you think that you are not ever going to get to the other side. But I will tell Mama some things that I am learning. I will do this because I know she will pay very close attention to what I say and she will be sad about what I teach her. I want her to be sad about genocide because I am sad about it. It will be good to have someone to talk about my feelings with.

But here are some more reasons I want my mother to come home. I want her to come here so she can see Maker again and do a lot of good cooking for us because she is the best cook in our family. And I want her to sit next to me the way Liliana sometimes does and smooth my prickly hair like she does not even mind that it pokes up.

Okay, I will write some more after I feed Hombre. He is very hungry, I think, because he is looking at me with sad eyes. Plus, he is wagging his tail and barking every time I lick the melted chocolate off the wrapper that had my candy bar in it. But I cannot give him chocolate because chocolate can kill dogs.

✳ ✳ ✳

I am back now to tell about what I learned today. But when I think about trying to write it all down, my thoughts sort of swim around in my head the way goldfish do if you leave them too long in one of those little plastic bags from the pet store.

Mr. Steinberg got us all to come to the front of the class today. We sat in a big circle. Then he asked us to talk about how we felt when we saw those things in the Holocaust Museum last week.

Everybody got real quiet. Except for Rusty White who was making his asthma wheeze sound like Darth Vadar. I know about Darth Vadar because Liliana let me watch *Star Wars* when I turned nine.

For a while, nobody said anything. Mostly we all looked out the big window in Mr. Steinberg's classroom at the rain that was falling. Today was the first very cold rain since last winter and I thought about the pictures I saw of the frozen skies at those horrible extermination camps in Poland. Those camps were covered in deep snow so white that it burned my eyes to look at them.

Finally, Cody Bracewell said that he did not like the new word that we were learning about. In fact, he said he hated the sound of it. Then he pinched Myra Das so hard that she made a croaking sound like frogs make after it rains.

Mr. Steinberg gave Cody a look that meant that he better behave. Then he went up to the chalkboard. He wrote *genocide* on the board. **He said, "Genocide. *Geno* comes from the Greek word *genos*. It means race. The *cide* part of the word is**

Latin and it means to kill. Now will someone in the class put the meaning of those word parts together?"

Rachel Ling whispered, "Race to kill."

Mr. Steinberg shook his head at us. "That's close, Rachel. Good try. Genocide means race killing. And yesterday, what race of people did you see Hitler and his Nazis killing?

I answered Mr. Steinberg's question. "The Jewish people most of all. But also the Gypsies and the Russians."

"And the handicapped people and the Polish people," Cody yelled out.

Mr. Steinberg said we were all right. Hitler had wanted to get rid of all of these groups of people. But he spent his biggest energies trying to make sure that the Jewish race of people would be exterminated. *Exterminate* means to totally wipe something out or get rid of it.

World War II had started when Hitler invaded Poland in 1939 and it did not end until 1945. It was a very big war that killed a lot of people (I think Mr. Steinberg said it was more than fifty five million). But before the war ended, a man named Raphael Lemkin made up the word genocide.

He made up the word in 1943, I think, but before that, he had studied a lot of history about race killing. Mr. Steinberg said that even when Raphael Lemkin was really young, that he was very smart. He spoke almost ten languages and he was very bothered by large groups of people getting slaughtered.

What made Raphael the most upset was there were not any laws that punished the kind of killing that Hitler and his Nazis did. **There were no laws that made leaders who destroyed groups of people have consequences for the horrible crimes that they had done.**

So Lemkin (who was a Jewish lawyer from Poland) spent his life working to make up laws that would help governments and leaders forbid and stop the killing of big groups of people. He made up a description of those awful things that happen when groups of people are destroyed. And he said that those crimes should not happen again. Besides this, he gave a name to those terrible things that destroy and kill people because of their race or religion or because of where they come from or because of their culture. The name he gave those things is *genocide.*

Eventually, Lemkin's hard work did some good. Mr. Steinberg said that after World War II, some of the Nazi leaders who had killed Jews and other people had to go to court in Nuremberg, Germany. From 1945 until 1946, many of the Nazi leaders were in this court called a *tribunal*. In the tribunal, the things that these Nazi leaders did were told to the court. At the end, these leaders were punished. Some were even sentenced to death. This was one of what Mr. Steinberg said was called the *Nuremberg Trials*. And this one that made the cruel leaders face their awful behaviors was called the *Trial of the Major Criminals*.

Anyway, Raphael was one of the people who worked to help get these trials ready. During the trials, the word "genocide" got used. But some more things still had to happen before a group of countries working together for world peace and security made an agreement about what genocide was and how it should be prevented and treated if it started to happen. The group of countries that did this is called the United Nations (or sometimes UN for short). I will tell you more about the United Nations when Mr. Steinberg tells us more.

But in December of 1948, this agreement that the United Nations adopted was mostly because of Raphael Lemkin's hard work. The agreement was called the *Genocide Convention*, and it got put in place to help make destroying groups of people something that countries all over the world would have to punish and prevent. Still, the Genocide Convention had to be approved or *ratified* by twenty UN members (for their own countries) to get turned into international law. *International law* just means the laws that countries all around the world have to pay attention to and obey.

On October 16, 1950, the twentieth country did this, and the Genocide Convention got turned into international law on January 12, 1951.

Mr. Steinberg said that Raphael Lemkin had spent his life doing very important work. He said that when we make it our business to protect the rights of people who cannot defend or protect themselves, we are doing a very good and right thing. Since Raphael worked to try and save people's lives, Mr. Steinberg said that he has left a great example for us to follow.

Mr. Steinberg showed us Raphael Lemkin's picture. He looked like a very nice man, all smart and serious with eyes that looked like he was telling the truth about things. Then our teacher put away Raphael's picture and we started talking about what we saw at the Holocaust Museum. We talked about how terrible things had been for the Jewish people. Mr. Steinberg told us more about concentration camps and also about those extermination camps in Poland. This was very hard. It was hard because we talked about the horrible ways that the people had been killed in these places. Some of the ways were so sick and awful that they made me want to put my fingers in my ears and make noises until Mr. Steinberg stopped talking. Rachel Ling bit her lip and then forgot to lick it. This made two drops of blood drip on her skirt. I know about these drips because I counted.

I will not write the details about the terrible ways so many people died during the Holocaust. But I will tell you that gas chambers are not for anything that is alive. No person should ever have died in one. And the horribleness of making people march and march in the rain and in the snow until they are so sick and tired that they cannot go anymore is something I cannot even describe.

But what is even worse about those awful marches is that this walking was often the last steps that the Jewish people would ever take.

Because even if a person managed to survive the marching, there was no way of escaping what usually came next.

CHAPTER 5

HEY J,

Today is my birthday. I am eleven now and this means that I am getting really grown up. Tonight we will have my favorite cake, which is chocolate with whipped cream frosting that has sprinkles on it. Maker gets to come over and eat some, too, because today is Wednesday.

Here is some other news: Yesterday a new president of America got elected. I have not written for two days because Mr. Steinberg said that so long as we write enough down, it is okay with him if we sometimes skip a few days. But yesterday, a man named Barack Obama got picked by the American people to be our next president.

At my school today, everybody talked about the election. This was probably because all the adults were just talking and talking about it.

A lot of people were very happy about Mr. Obama being our next president. But there were some people who seemed cranky about it.

Mr. Steinberg says this is the way a democracy works. Our government is made up of and by the American people. It is set up so that we get to choose who our leaders are. We do this choosing by voting. And mostly every American citizen who is old enough can vote for the people that they want to be their leaders. I am not old enough to vote.

Anyway, some Americans did not vote for Barack Obama yesterday. But more of them did vote for him than the people who did not. So next year, in January, I think, Mr. Obama and his wife and daughters will move into the White House.

I am excited about Mr. Obama. He seems good and fair. But the other man in the election seemed good and fair, too. So I wish that they both could have won because that would mean no one had to lose. And I am sure that the other man who wanted to be the president feels a little sad right now.

Still, I think democracy is a very good idea because the people of America choose their leaders and the leaders have to answer to the people. Mr. Steinberg says this is very healthy because it keeps one or two people from being totally in charge and doing unfair or bad things like Hitler did.

So I am happy about Mr. Obama, and I am hoping that he and his family like Washington, D.C.

I am also happy about my birthday cake that we will eat tonight. I can smell it baking in the oven right now and this is because Lili did not have time to make it before she went to one of her little study groups earlier today.

Speaking of today, Mr. Steinberg told us again that he would be teaching us about a bunch of genocides that have happened in the past one hundred years. He said that genocides have happened for thousands of years and that we could talk about those from very ancient civilizations. We could talk about many other race killings that have happened. But he said that we would stick to genocides that have happened in the past century.

Mr. Steinberg also said that we were going to talk about some ways that we can help stop genocide. And we will learn about some of the things that help cause race killing. My teacher said that understanding exactly why genocides happen is very complicated—and that there are not very many easy answers.

But he said that we cannot use this as an excuse for not trying to help. And he told us that there is a thing that everyone can do when it comes to helping end genocide.

Sophia Mandola asked Mr. Steinberg to say some more about this. She asked how a kid who is in fifth grade or a goofy teenager like her big brother could do things that would help end killings of thousands—or even millions—of people.

Mr. Steinberg gave our class a little smile that made his moustache twitch. It made him look sort of like a mouse. I like mice a lot. Then he said, "The word for what we're studying these next few weeks, boys and girls, is genocide. You already know this. You've already seen some of the horror that comes with this most terrible crime against humans. And over the next couple of weeks, you'll learn more."

Then Mr. Steinberg scooted some papers off the side of his desk and he sat down while he finished talking to us.

"As you learn, boys and girls, you will become witnesses. Usually a witness is a person who has seen something for him or herself. But there are other kinds of witnesses, too. And these are people who study and learn from the past—or even the present. Maybe these people have not actually seen things like the Holocaust, but they choose to learn from history and research and the experiences of people who have survived such times."

Somebody—I do not know who because I was chewing my pencil and this made some fun crunching noises in my ears— asked what a witness can do.

Mr. Steinberg wrinkled up his forehead. He does this a lot when he is thinking. Then he said, "Witnesses who care about others can do great good in this world. When people learn about bad or unfair things happening and then choose to use their voices to say what's true for those who cannot defend themselves, they are bearing witness. They are doing the work of helping end something wrong and unjust. And in so doing they make their lives count for things much bigger than themselves."

I liked the sound of all of this. It made me feel important. It made me think that even though I am only eleven and I am not the new President of the United States, that I can do something good. I might even help people who are having very hard times. So I asked Mr. Steinberg to tell us exactly what we could do to help stop genocide. I asked him if there are any genocides now and, if there are, how could we help end them?

I think my teacher liked my question because he winked at me. Mr. Steinberg usually only winks at us when we pay such good attention that we get all of his questions right during our Friday game of Social Studies Charades.

"Yes, Javier, there is a genocide happening right now in a place called Darfur. Darfur is in the western region of Sudan. Sudan is the largest country on the continent of Africa. We will definitely be talking about Darfur. And we will be learning ways that each of you can get involved in helping stop genocide. But remember this for now: Everyone can do *something*. There is a thing each of us can do to help bring about good change." Then

Mr. Steinberg stood up and pushed around some more papers on his desk. He gave all of us a very serious look. "But it's not enough for us to just know this, class. If things are going to be different, we have to get involved and do the thing that we can do."

Do the thing that we can do. **I am thinking about this idea of Mr. Steinberg's right now.**

I like it. It must mean that a smart and good man like Mr. Steinberg thinks that even kids can help bad things in faraway places get better.

So when I figure out whatever thing I can do to help, I might tell Maker about genocide and see if he wants to help, too.

Maybe if everybody did something, genocides could stop and kids all over the world could be safe. And Liliana says that living in a safe place is one of the best things that can happen to a person.

CHAPTER 6

HELLO JOURNAL,

Remember I told you we would be talking about a bunch of genocides that happened in the past one hundred years? Well, I was wrong. Today Mr. Steinberg wrote down all of the genocides we will learn about. He told us to copy them off the board so we could write about them in our journals. And there are only six we will study.

He said we had learned about the Holocaust first. This is because our human history had never had the kind of huge killings that were planned and carried out like those that happened when Hitler ruled Germany.

But Mr. Steinberg said that this was the order of the genocides we would study from the past one hundred years:

Armenia – this one happened during the years 1915–1918
The Holocaust – which we already studied; it happened during the years 1938–1945
Cambodia – this one happened from 1975 until 1979
Bosnia – this genocide happened from 1992 until 1995
Rwanda – this one happened so quickly—just one hundred days in 1994!
Darfur – this one began in 2003 and it is still going on, but Mr. Steinberg said that this genocide is connected to other horrible things that have happened in Sudan since 1983

The reason I can write all of this down so easily is because I worked hard to take notes so I could write them here. So I am looking at my sheet of notes right now. Otherwise, I could not remember the stuff I am supposed to write about.

Here is something else Mr. Steinberg said we had to know: He said there were other genocides that have happened during the past one hundred years—and there were definitely a lot that had happened further back in our history as humans. He said the terrible killing in 1988 of over 180,000 Kurdish people in northern Iraq had been a genocide. A very cruel leader named Saddam Hussein had ordered his Iraqi army and government to kill the Kurdish people and destroy the places where they lived. He also said the Nanking Massacre and the awful killings in a place called East Timor had been genocide. He said that the Transatlantic Slave Trade that happened from the 1400s through the mid-1800s had caused at least twelve million African people to be captured and made into slaves (even tens of millions more were killed or died before they ever started to work as slaves). This had been the work of a genocide, Mr. Steinberg said, even though the plan was not to kill, but to make the people into slaves.

He also said that we once had genocide behavior in the United States!

I thought that maybe I had some wax stuck in my left ear again (sometimes my ears get all full of wax and Liliana makes me clean them out) and that I was hearing wrong. But Mr. Steinberg said that when settlers came to North America, they began to make the Native Americans (Native Americans are also called Indians) move to other places. The poor Indians had to leave their homes and their villages and go where the new government sent them. The Indians were made to march (like the Jews had to do). They were starved and treated worse than animals by some of the new people who settled here. Because of this, millions of them died. And this had been their land in the first place!

Oh, and listen to this: There was another kind of genocide that happened in Canada. It started in the 1800s and it did not really end until 1996! What happened was the government of Canada made a bunch of schools and forced the aboriginal people of Canada (those of the First Nations, Inuit and Metis groups) to send their children to them. These schools were run by different churches, and the children who went there had to live at the schools. They could not go home to their families. This was because the government said that these aboriginal children (they are also known as Indians) needed to be like other Canadians who were not Indian. So the children could not speak the language of their people and could not practice their own beliefs about life and faith. If they did, they were badly hurt by the people in charge of them.

These residential schools in Canada caused thousands of children to die. Mr. Steinberg said that many of these deaths happened because the children got killed by disease and terrible treatment. The religious people who ran the schools sometimes did awful things to the children. Sometimes they even killed them.

In June of 2008, Canada's prime minister, who is named Stephen Harper, made a big apology for all of the awful things done to the aboriginal people of Canada.

Mr. Steinberg said that some of these terrible things that have happened to groups of people might not be called genocide. This is so even though a lot of people in a group might be severely hurt or killed. He said that sometimes there is confusion about what bad things make up a genocide.

In the Genocide Convention that Raphael Lemkin helped make in 1948, genocide is "doing any of these following things with the plan of destroying—either completely or partly—a national, ethnic, racial or religious group of people":

a. *Killing members of the group*

b. *Causing serious harm to the bodies or minds of the people in a group*

c. *Creating an environment for the group that is meant to bring about its physical destruction—either completely or partly*

d. *Doing things that keep babies from being born in the group*

e. *Forcing children of the group to be moved to another group of people* *

I know all this definition stuff and these lists looks like something out of a big text book, but Mr. Steinberg said we needed to have these things in our journals. To make stuff easier for us kids though, he said that he was giving us easier

---

* Paraphrase of Article 2 of the 1948 Convention on the Prevention and Punishment of the Crime of Genocide

language than the definition in the Genocide Convention. He said that this definition is important and that we might even have a test on it.

I detest tests. Detest is a word that I learned from Carmen. She uses it instead of saying the word "hate" because Papa won't let us say "hate."

Anyway, I copied down stuff today, like the order of the genocides we will study and this definition of genocide. But tomorrow I promise to be more normal and just tell you stuff that I learn about Armenia.

Now I will go to sleep. But first I will eat the last piece of my chocolate birthday cake from last night. I will drink cold milk with it then put my pajamas on and get into bed without brushing my teeth.

Liliana is at another one of her study groups and she is not home to check my teeth before I go to sleep.

I am glad because I also detest brushing my teeth.

CHAPTER 7

NOVEMBER 12, 2008

HI J,

I am back but I only want to write a little bit. Plus, I'm bored with just telling you this-is-this and that-is-that about genocide.

This is probably because I am creative. I know that I am creative because Liliana says so and so does Carmen. And Carmen does not pay any attention to me except to tell me to get out of the room that she and Liliana share.

So I must be creative, and because this is true, I am going to tell you about the genocide in Armenia like it is a story in a book.

Javier's True Story About Genocide in Armenia

Once upon a time, in an area between the Black and Caspian Seas that is now called the Caucasus, very bad things started to happen. The place where these things happened is right at the cross of three continents: Asia, Africa and Europe.

Anyway, for maybe three thousand years, some people had lived in the south part of this area and they had their own country. This country had been called Armenia and the people who lived there were the Armenians. But by the end of the 1800s, this land was ruled by a big empire called the Ottoman Empire. This empire was sometimes called the Turkish Empire or Turkey.

But the Ottoman Empire with its Turkish armies (this means armies made up of soldiers from Turkey) was getting weak. Even though this empire had once been very powerful, a lot of countries that had been made to be part of it got to be free.

But the Armenians — they were not so lucky. They had to be under the rule of a fierce sultan named Sultan Abdul Hamid. Sultan Hamid's special armies killed around 200,000 Armenian people. These big killing sprees were called pogroms (like the pogroms that hurt and killed Jewish people during the Holocaust). And they happened when the Armenians started asking for a more fair government. The Armenians also wanted ways of doing things that did not punish them for believing differently about God than the sultan and his followers did.

But some modern thinking leaders in the Turkish army called the Young Turks started changing stuff (the Young Turks were also known as the Committee of Union and Progress, or CUP for short). In 1908, they took power away from the sultan and began to allow a government that was more fair. These changes seemed like they might help Turkey get better in many ways!

Now the Armenian people were much happier. So were the Turkish people.

But this does not end happily ever after because some greedy and very radical Young Turks took full power of the government in 1913. And they stole the power by this thing called a coup d'etat. A coup d'etat means a little group (usually) forces out a country's government and puts itself in charge.

So the three radical Young Turks (their names were Mehmed Talaat, Enver Pasha and Djemal Pasha) got rid of the old leaders and made themselves have all the power. And like Hitler, they liked their power and wanted some more of it. They wanted Turkey to get bigger so they could be in control of more lands and people. They wanted to make a new and bigger Turkish empire. They wanted to call this empire Turan and they wanted it to have only one religion and one language.

This was not good because Armenia's original land was right in the way of the three Young Turks' plan to get bigger by going east and doing their conquering.

And on the land that they wanted to take over was about two million Armenian people! These Armenians were Christians. This means that the Armenians followed the teachings of Jesus Christ. The Young Turks were not Christians. They were

Muslim and their religion was Islam, which meant that they followed the teachings of their prophet, Mohammed. The Young Turks, especially Mehmed Talaat, did not like Christians.

The Young Turks' plan about the new and bigger land of Turan, plus their very dramatic way of following their religion, led them to begin killing the Armenian people. They began doing this because they wanted the land. They also did not like it that the Armenians did not believe the same things that they did about God.

Oh, I almost forgot—a lot of the Armenians were very educated. They were doctors and lawyers and business people. The Turks were not. Mostly, they were peasant farmers or they owned little stores. Most did not have much education at all. And they did not want a government that let citizens share their ideas or vote. The Turks would not have liked our democracy here in America. But I bet the Armenians would have!

So the Young Turks started pointing out all the differences between their religion and the Armenians to other Turks. They made a big deal about the differences between their culture and ways of doing things compared to the ways that the Armenians did things. Like the anti-Semitic propaganda that the Nazis used to get non-Jewish people to hate the Jews, the Young Turks worked hard to make other Turks think bad things about Armenian people. But just like many German people did not like the plan of Hitler and his Nazis, there must have been some Turkish people who did not have hate or prejudice for the Armenians.

Now this next thing is terrible. But also like Hitler did, a war was used to cover up the awful things that the Young Turks began to do to the Armenians. World War I started in 1914, and the Young Turk leaders were on the side of the Central Powers (this means the countries of Germany and Austria-Hungary). They joined in the fight against against the Allied Powers of Britain, France and Russia.

Well, the poor Armenians were stuck in the middle for real! They lived right between Russia and Turkey, so they begged Turkey not to fight their neighbor, Russia. The Armenians also said that they would not help with a Turkish plan to fight against Russia.

The Turks now said that Armenians were helping out their Russian enemy, so in January of 1915, while the Central and Allied Powers did their fighting against each other, the Turks started taking away the weapons that the Armenian people had. Now the Armenians could not defend themselves.

Thousands of Armenian men who were in the Turkish army had their weapons taken away by Turks. Then they got turned into slaves. These Armenian men got forced to work like animals until they died. If they did not die soon enough, the Turks shot them with guns.

In April of 1915, the three cruel Young Turks sent telegrams to the country leaders all over Turkey. In the telegrams were orders written in a secret code. The orders commanded the country leaders to kill all Armenians.

On April 24th, the Turkish soldiers gathered and killed a group of Armenian men who were very strong and smart leaders among their people. There were about 250 of them at first (but that number got up to around 600), and they were killed in a city called Constantinople. Constantinople is now named Istanbul. Then the Turks got huge groups of other men together. They killed those men violently, too.

Next, the Turkish soldiers made the Armenian women and children and old people leave their houses. This was like the Jewish people being taken away to the concentration camps because these Armenians were tricked, too! They were told they were being moved to safer places and even to bring a few things with them.

But what was really happening was the Turks were taking over all of the Armenians' homes and their things. This stealing was taking place while the Armenian people were being forced to walk hundreds of miles, many times into the desert of Syria.

This walking was like the death marches that the Jews went on before they were killed. Often, the Armenians were forced to walk and walk for miles and miles. They ran out of food and the Turkish soldiers, villagers and some criminals who had already done horrible crimes, did terrible and sickening things to the women and girls who were forced on these walks. And if the people got tired and fell down, the soldiers beat them until they got up and walked again.

Most of the Armenians died during these marches so there were dead bodies everywhere. Some of the Armenian women got to choose between being killed and marrying a Turkish man. If they decided to marry, then they also had to become a follower of the Muslim religion. They could not be Christians anymore.

Even though other parts of the world began to learn about this genocide, nothing was done to make the killings stop. Some people did care, though. Here in the United States, the horribleness of what was happening got reported a lot in a big newspaper called the *New York Times*. Also, Britain, France and Russia warned the Young Turks that there would be big trouble if they kept up the killings. Some Protestant missionaries were very helpful and kind to Armenian survivors, and the American ambassador to the Ottoman Empire kept saying how bad these killings were. I think his name was Henry Morgenthau, and he really spoke up for the Armenians.

But no real help came to the Armenians from the outside world. In 1918, the war ended and the Central Powers lost. Just before it ended, the three Young Turks ran away to Germany because they knew they would have to go to court and be on trial for all of their evilness. And because Germany did not send them back to face their wrong, some people went looking for those three Young Turks who planned the genocide. I think at least two of them got found and killed. I know for sure that Mehmed Talaat did.

There is no happy ending to this story because a lot of Armenian people died—at least a million, and maybe even more than 1.5 million. Then after the people were all dead, the Turks went back and destroyed whole Armenian cities. Libraries and very old records from the past were ruined. Buildings that had been built hundreds of years ago (and maybe even thousands), all got completely wiped out by the Turks.

And when you make a whole history of somebody or some group go away, it is very hard to remember what you are not supposed to forget.

CHAPTER 8

HI J,

Today I am in a very BAD MOOD!
Mama will not be coming to Washington, D.C. after all.
Papa says this is because she cannot get all the papers she needs
to come here settled soon enough. So she will not come.

I do not care about stupid papers. I want my mother to come
and spend time with me. I told Papa this. I even used the word
stupid because I did not care if he got mad at me.

But he did not get mad. He was patient with me even though
I know that the work that he does in his big building made him
very tired today.

So after I said *stupid*, he gave a big sigh and told me to sit
down beside him. Then he told me that he understood how sad
and disappointed I must feel. He even said that he was feeling
a little sad himself.

But Papa said that the papers that Mama needed to come
here were not stupid. When people from one country move to
another country, or even when they just visit another country,
there are certain rules that must be followed. The rules are put
in place to protect everybody. They are there to keep countries
as safe and organized as possible.

Papa said that we had come to the United States from Mexico as *immigrants*. He said an immigrant is a person who leaves
his country to settle permanently in another country. And he
said that there are different ways that immigrants come to new
countries.

Since I did not know about these ways, and since I was just
finding out that I was an immigrant (even though I did not

feel very much like an immigrant), I asked him about the ways people can come to new countries to live.

Papa said that this is complicated since there are so many reasons that people choose to *emigrate* or leave their homelands. But he said there is a legal way to immigrate, which means that an immigrant would follow all of the rules to come into a new country. And there is another way that an immigrant could come to a country—and this way meant that the person coming might ignore or not follow some of the rules.

Papa said that when we came here, we had done everything the way that the United States government asks. And now we are citizens or permanent residents of the United States. Even though this had taken a lot of time, and Papa had to fill out a lot of papers for me, my sisters, my brother (before he was killed) and himself, he had wanted to do the right thing and follow the rules.

And when Mama comes to visit, he said we would always follow the rules.

I asked Papa why Mama could not come and still follow all of the rules to travel here. Papa said that they had decided for her to come a little bit too late. They should have started making plans for her visit earlier. Because they had not begun earlier, certain documents would not be ready in time for her to be here for Christmas.

I have not seen my Mama since my brother, Sergio, died in the war two years ago. She was here for his funeral and that was a terrible time. Everyone cried and forgot to make food for me to eat. I think that I cried, too, but mostly my stomach had hurt a lot and I just wanted to play with my toys and sleep.

Now, I will not see my mother during the happy time of Christmas and the New Year. And even though I think that Papa is right, and that we need to follow all the rules, I still want my Mama to be here.

So I am in a bad mood.

Another reason I am not very happy is that we talked some more about genocide today. I am tired of genocide now, and we still have four more genocides to learn about.

But the reason I am so upset is that Mr. Steinberg was explaining how these awful things get to keep happening.

He said in Turkey, which was where the Armenian genocide happened, the Turkish leaders still keep denying that genocide ever happened. *Deny* means to say that something is not so. And the Turkish government says that there was no genocide of the Armenian people almost one hundred years ago.

Mr. Steinberg said that when genocides get ignored by other countries, or when leaders of countries committing genocide get away with these terrible crimes against their people, the genocide gets to keep happening. He said that right now this is happening in Sudan. He said we will talk more about Sudan later. We will talk about the part of Sudan where genocide is happening. This place is called Darfur.

My teacher also said that ignoring genocide is wrong. He said that genocide mostly got ignored in Armenia and it got ignored during the Holocaust for a very long time. People knew about the terrible things happening.

But many did not do anything to stop the awful crimes.

He said that when people know about these things and do nothing, they are *watchers*. They watch and hear about the bad things that are happening. But they do not get involved.

He said that when people know about these things and *do* try to help, they are *doers*.

Mr. Steinberg said that since genocide is like an enormous giant, none of us know exactly how to make it end. The problem with this is that the leaders and people who are helping create a genocide know this. They know that there are many government leaders and people who will just watch while genocide gets planned and put into action.

These leaders know that they will get to do terrible things to the people they want to hurt and kill.

And nobody will do much to stop them.

This getting away with bad things without any consequence is called *impunity*, Mr. Steinberg told us.

Ahmed Naghavi asked Mr. Steinberg what could be done about impunity and Mr. Steinberg said that this was a great question.

"Impunity ends when watchers stand up and become doers," he told our class. "When the leaders who plan genocides against groups of people have to face consequences for their wrong, they will think twice before starting genocides. When they know that doers will take action and get involved instead of just ignoring or watching the terrible crimes, they will hesitate to begin a genocide."

Rachel Ling asked about the laws that would help prevent genocides from happening again—those laws that Raphael Lemkin had worked to get into place. Didn't the Genocide Convention help protect people from genocides?

Mr. Steinberg said that even though many world leaders know about past genocides in Armenia and Europe and other places, they have not paid attention to the Genocide Convention like they should do. He said that in his opinion, there is too much talk about what makes up a genocide and not enough action to stop or prevent one in the first place. The Genocide Convention helps make many things about genocide clear. It also talks about preventing and punishing this terrible crime. But different countries and world leaders have to *choose to get involved and help stop genocide*. When the leaders in countries know about genocide in another country, they have to speak up and start working to make it end.

I asked Mr. Steinberg to tell us some of the countries that might want to help. First, he told us about the countries that had agreed with and signed onto what the Genocide Convention said. Then, he asked if we remembered that big group of countries that work together for peace and development and security around the world. He told us that this group is called the *United Nations* (or UN for short) and that many countries that are in the UN had been responsible for helping get the Genocide Convention all situated.

I sort of remembered the United Nations and I think some of the other kids did, too. But I could tell that we did not really remember much—not even Ahmed—because everybody stayed real quiet.

"The United Nations came about after the Second World War," Mr. Steinberg told us. "It started in 1945 with just fifty countries that got together to create the United Nations Charter. A *charter* is a written explanation that tells why a group is being formed, what the group will do and how it will do what it says it will. So the fifty countries figured all this out together based on some other good work and ideas that had existed before. Then they all signed the UN Charter. A little later, Poland signed the Charter, too, and became one of the original fifty-one member states. Now there are 192 countries that make up the UN."

"So what does the UN do," I asked, "and how could they help make genocides stop?"

Mr. Steinberg said that he has a really smart class that asks a lot of good questions. This made me feel proud of myself because I was the one who had asked the smart question.

"Well, there is a part of the UN called the Security Council," he explained. "This Council has fifteen members from different countries around the world. Five of these members are permanent, which means that they stay the same. These permanent members are the countries of the United Kingdom, Russia, the United States, China and France. The other ten countries switch out or rotate. They get to work on the Security Council for two years, and they get chosen based on the region of the world where they come from. But the purpose of this UN Security Council is to keep world peace, and if the peace of a country is in danger, the Council can and should get involved."

"I get it," Rusty White practically yelled, and even though I got it too, I just stayed quiet because Rusty hardly ever gets anything except detention. This is mostly because he makes himself busy doing vexing stuff to everyone in the class. I know about vexing because sometimes I use my vexing skills to frustrate Carmen. "That Security Council could call on members of that United Nations group to take some action. Right?"

"Exactly," said Mr. Steinberg.

"Yeah, they could make up a big fat war and get all the countries to go in and blow up the bad country making the genocide against those groups of people. They could send in a zillion war planes and drop bombs..."

"Rusty," interrupted our teacher, "I just explained that the UN Security Council is in place to help solve problems in the world. It exists to make peace and provide security. Using force to help end genocide might actually have to happen in some of these countries. Peacekeeping forces that go into areas where war is happening and where people cannot protect themselves can be a very appropriate option. But the UN does not 'go in and blow up anything or anyone.'"

Then our teacher explained that the Security Council works for *peaceful* ways to end genocide. He said that we do our best to use something called *diplomacy* to handle problems. I think this means that groups and countries that don't agree about stuff do their best to keep acting nicely and talking about things instead of doing what Rusty said. **But my teacher said that if all of these efforts fail, the UN Security Council should definitely stand up and take the actions that are best for the situation. He said that this might mean deploying peacekeeping troops that have certain orders to protect the people who are being hurt.** Lots of soldiers all working together are called *troops*, and *deploy* means to organize or get troops together to take action.

Mr. Steinberg said that not enough action in the past is one of the biggest reasons why genocide is happening in the present. And if more watching and no doing keeps happening, genocides will continue in the future.

This sounds very bad to me.

"Impunity can no longer be an option," Mr. Steinberg said to us as the bell rang and we grabbed our stuff to go. "Having no immediate consequences for killing thousands—and even millions—of people is probably the greatest cause of modern day genocide."

This sounds right to me. Sometimes I obey Papa only because I know what will happen if I do not. And I know that I am not a leader in a government or anything like that, but if I was, and if I knew that the UN Security Council really meant serious business about stopping genocide, I would behave myself and not make plans to start a genocide.

In the meantime, I have decided that I do not want to be a watcher and I do not want the leaders of my country, America, to just be watchers.

I want to be a doer. Even if I do not know what this means yet.

CHAPTER 9

DEAR J,

I have decided to write only a page today. The reason why is because I am thinking about Christmas right now even if it is still a long time away. I am thinking about the cookies Liliana will make and the tamales we will have on Christmas Eve. I am thinking about how I will not have to go to school for two whole weeks.

And I do not think that Christmas and genocide go together. One is a happy thing to talk about. And one is so sad that it sometimes makes it hard for me to breathe.

So tonight I will think some more about Christmas and I will not think about race killing. I will not think about the genocide that we studied in class today. The one that happened on the continent of Asia in a country named Cambodia.

But I will tell you this: I think that all of those people who got killed in Armenia and Poland and Cambodia and other places are like ghosts that do scary dances.

Because sometimes after I turn off my light and try to go to sleep, I can almost see them. They twirl and curl around the way blue smoke rising up from a burning cigarette does. I know about curling smoke because sometimes Carmen's friend, Santiago, sneaks his Papa's cigarettes and smokes them on our porch.

But the genocide ghosts are different than just plain smoke. They have faces that twist up and look very sad and scared. They have bodies that start out normal. But then they stretch and get skinnier and skinnier until they are so thin that they just fade away.

The ghosts are all different just like the people who died in these genocides were. But the thing that they all have in common is this: All of them look like people. And all of them twist and turn in this ugly dance before they just fade away to nothing.

CHAPTER 10

HELLO J,

I guess I better write about Cambodia today.
But I would prefer to put this book away;
And maybe pray;
Because now the world seems extra gray.
And with everything that happened
It seems like someone should pay.
Okay, I am done with my poem. I know it is stupid, but I
wrote it because it is mostly how I feel. Plus, I do not want to
write about what happened in Cambodia. It is terrible just like
Armenia and the Holocaust was. All race killing is terrible.

It should stop.

I know. I will become a ninja. I will get Maker to be a
ninja, too. We will create a secret ninja club that makes a web
all around the world. And we will all use our ninja powers to
spy out genocides. Then we will use our martial arts and ninja
skills to interrupt all the bad things. We will dress in black and
scare the leaders who are causing genocides so badly that they
will stop the killing and behave themselves. But we will not do
any assassinations. Because then we would only be adding to the
killing, except in a different, sort of opposite-like way.

Or maybe that UN Security Council should just do its job
and protect people in countries where the leaders are trying to
hurt them. They need to remind all of the countries that signed
that Genocide Convention that when there is a genocide, those
countries all said that they would get involved.

Yeah. That is what should happen. That UN Security Council should do what it is supposed to do. They should work to-

gether to give peace and protection to places in the world that need it.

Then Maker and I will not need to be ninjas.

So here is some news about what happened in Cambodia. Cambodia is far away from Washington, D.C. It is in Asia, right in between the countries of Thailand and Vietnam.

So in the country of Cambodia, there were lots of problems after it got to be free from France being in charge of it. This happened completely in 1954. Then Cambodia got to be ruled by a leader named Prince Norodom Sihanouk.

Meanwhile, there was another man named Saloth Sar. He was born in Cambodia and he had gone away to France to study. But instead of learning about the subject he planned to, he got interested in Communism. Communism is a kind of government where only one small group has power and this group controls pretty much everything.

When Saloth Sar came back to Cambodia, he got involved in a secret Communist group. He changed his name to Pol Pot. Pol Pot means "Original Cambodian" and it was a name that Saloth Sar picked because he wanted to hide that he was actually a rich person. Also, he was very prejudiced against people who he thought were not true Cambodians.

Pol Pot became leader of the Cambodian Communist Party (CCP) although he was not in charge of Cambodia. Prince Sihanouk was still the head of the country. But in the early 1960s, Pol Pot had to flee to the jungle so he could escape the Prince's anger. In the jungle Pol Pot got an army together to make a war against the Prince's government. The army was called the Khmer Rouge.

But stuff changed in 1970 when a man named General Lon Nol stole the government from Prince Sihanouk (Mr. Steinberg told us that the United States had helped support this). Now Lon Nol was in charge and he liked the United States and did not like Vietnam—and Vietnam was where the United States was fighting a war.

Between the years of 1969 and 1973, United States planes dropped more than a half million tons of bombs in the country part of Cambodia. About 150,000 Cambodian peasants (*peasants* are people who usually live in the country and are small farmers of land) got killed. This happened because Cambodia is right next to Vietnam and the American soldiers were trying to get to places where they thought the Vietnamese fighters were staying. So the American soldiers attacked parts of Cambodia. All of this fighting was so scary that it made a lot of the peasant Cambodian people run toward a city called Phnom Penh. Phnom Penh is the capital of Cambodia.

Now, all of this trouble and confusion, plus the fact that the United States had supported getting Prince Sihanouk kicked out and replaced by General Nol, gave Pol Pot a lot of encouragement from the people. Pol Pot was in charge of the Khmer Rouge, which was an army made up of mostly peasant teenage boys. This Communist army did not like the way that people in the West (this mostly means Europe and the United States) lived their lives. They detested Western culture and wanted to clean away the Western ideas and ways of life that had become part of Cambodia.

So on April 17, 1975, Pol Pot and the Khmer Rouge army went into the city of Phnom Penh and conquered it. By this time, the Vietnam War was over and the American soldiers were not in Vietnam or Cambodia anymore. Now the country was renamed Democratic Kampuchea and Pol Pot was in charge.

Immediately, Pol Pot began using his power to do very bad things.

Right away, he started doing things that he had learned about from a very harsh leader in China named Mao Zedong. Since Pol Pot had visited China and China was also Communist, he had learned about Mao's plan called the "Great Leap Forward." This was not a plan about making good jumps ahead or anything. This plan of Mao's that Pol Pot copied in Cambodia was one that was supposed to cause the country to grow quickly by making the people who farm do very hard work to produce good crops. Crops make money when they get sold and the money makes the country richer.

Pol Pot wanted to copy this plan that also meant that people who lived in cities got forced to go into the country to work. He wanted everyone to be peasants, everyone to have the same things and he wanted everyone to be a Communist.

So he closed off the country from all outside ideas and ways of living. There were no more people from other countries allowed inside of Cambodia. There was no more radio or newspapers or television allowed. There were no more schools or factories or hospitals. Even mail got stopped—and money was all taken away. Can you believe it? There was no money anymore!

With Pol Pot in charge, the Cambodian people did not have any rights at all. They had to do exactly what he and his Khmer Rouge army said to do. The people could not even say what they thought anymore and there was no more religion allowed. This was very hard because most of the people were Buddhist, and Buddhist people definitely have a religious way of living. But if the Cambodian people disobeyed even a little bit, they were immediately killed.

The Khmer Rouge made the people leave the cities of Cambodia and march toward the countryside where they would have to be peasant farmers. Two million people got marched out of Phnom Penh. Around 20,000 of those people died as they walked and walked. This was probably because the journey to the country lasted about six weeks. The walking was like the horrible walking the Armenians had to do and like the Jews having to march. This was so awful.

The people who lived got made into slaves. Just like the Nazis made the Jews work like slaves in the concentration camps, the Khmer Rouge forced the Cambodian people to work and work in the rice fields. If they ate any of the crops they were harvesting, they got killed in awful, cruel ways. These Cambodian people all had to live together in large groups and work eighteen hours every day.

Soon a lot more people died because they were starved and had to work too hard. They got sick and there were no doctors to help them get well. The Khmer Rouge soldiers did not care. They gave the Cambodian people only the tiniest amounts of food and practically no rest at all. It did not matter to these cruel men that the people kept dying.

The Cambodian people were treated like the Jewish people in the ghettos. Then, in a lot of ways, they got treated like the Jews in the concentration and death camps.

The Khmer Rouge gathered up and killed people who had been government leaders before Pol Pot was in charge. They killed citizens who were educated and people who were rich. They murdered Buddhist monks, policemen, teachers, doctors and lawyers. This was like the leaders in Armenia who were killed in Constantinople by the Young Turks.

These horrible killings happened with weapons like guns, axe handles, spades or sometimes sharp bamboo sticks.

Pol Pot and his army wanted "pure" Cambodians and all of these people were not "pure" in his mind. This was like Hitler's very prejudiced thinking about Jews being inferior and Germans being the perfect race. Except that Pol Pot and his Khmer helpers were Cambodians—and so were a lot of the people they were killing.

Other people who got killed were Chinese people, Vietnamese people and people from Thailand. Also Cham Muslim people got murdered. Cham is short for Champa and the Cham people are descendants of the ancient Kingdom of Champa. A lot of Cham people live in southeast Asia.

Besides the horrible places in the countryside, there were detention centers in the big cities of Cambodia. In these centers, Khmer Rouge soldiers tortured the people who were brought there. The people who came had not done anything wrong. But since the Khmer Rouge's job was to extinguish the old society and get rid of traitors, they killed people for reasons that were made up and not true. Some of the people who were killed were even soldiers who worked for the Khmer Rouge!

The people who went to these centers were not usually killed there unless they died from disease, torture or from starvation. Instead, these Cambodian prisoners of the Khmer Rouge got taken to open fields. There, they got executed in horrible ways and then dumped into enormous graves. These places where killings and burials happened got called the "killing fields."

The most terrible center was in the city of Phnom Penh. It was an old high school named Tuol Sleng before it became a place called S-21. The leader of this awful center was a man named Kaing Guek Eav or "Duch." S-21 became known as the place where the people go in but they never come out. This is because somewhere between 14,000 and 20,000 prisoners went into this center. But they never came out.

Instead, they got asked a lot of questions by Khmer Rouge leaders and then they were tortured in unbelievable ways. I would tell you these terrible ways except that they make my stomach sick to think about them. Then the people got executed by the Khmer soldiers, who were mostly teenagers (I think I already said this, but it creeps me out to think that some of the people who did these awful things were just a little older than me).

Mr. Steinberg said that S-21 is now a genocide museum.

The evilness of Cambodia started to end in December of 1978 when Vietnam invaded the country. A couple of weeks later, that big city of Phnom Penh got taken over. Pol Pot lost his power. He went away to a distant part of the country near Thailand. There he kept trying to get his Khmer Rouge army to fight against the Cambodian governments that came next.

Pol Pot died in 1998 and he never had to face his horrible, terrible, mean crimes that killed almost two million people (Mr. Steinberg said 1.7 million, but he thought it could be more).

Some Khmer Rouge leaders are supposed to answer for their crimes even though it has been more than thirty years since this happened. That group called the United Nations is supporting a tribunal that will soon make some of these leaders face the cruel things that they did—things that killed nearly two million people.

If you ask me, these brutal men should have had to face their awful choices way before now.

Raphael Lemkin was right. There should definitely be laws against race killing. **And even though we have some, the rules seem sort of like my old blue comb that has almost all of its teeth missing.**

So just like my hair does not get combed all good and straight (this is maybe why it sticks up), the bad people who plan and make genocides get to hang around and get away with their crimes for a very long time.

CHAPTER 11

HELLLLLLOOOOO JJJJJJJJ,

I am being very weird today. But this is okay. Because I do have something to say.

The first thing is that today is December! Last week was Thanksgiving and now we are back at school and our winter break is going to come very soon. I am glad about these holidays for a bunch of reasons. But I am too tired to tell the reasons now.

Anyway, last Thursday, me and my family spent Thanksgiving with Maker and his family. I ate too many of the empanadas Lili made and this made me spend time in the bathroom, which was not very fun.

But I am not in the bathroom now. I am in my room and I have to tell you something.

I saw some things that I should not have seen after school today. Actually, Maker and I saw these things together. Later, I will probably have to tell Papa about what happened because what I saw was very confusing.

I will not tell Liliana because she is busy studying for some big tests called final exams. When she studies for these, she forgets to answer me when I talk to her. Instead, she just makes some little noises and chews on her pen. This is how I learned to chew pens—by watching Lili do it.

I will not tell Carmen because she is in her room burping. She does this all of the time now because she and her friends have burping contests to see who can make the loudest and longest burps. But she can only do this when Papa is not home and Lili is so busy that she forgets to tell Carmen to stop it. Once Papa gets home, there is no more burping to be done. He says young ladies do not burp and that Carmen is going to be a young lady, not a troublesome burper.

I do not say anything, but I think that Carmen *is* a troublesome burper... and a lot of other things, too. And I do not think that she is a young lady at all. She is more like a young beast.

Anyway, today was a good day at school. I got my report card. I had all A's, which is pretty normal for me. My teachers said nice things about me, too. Things like "Javier always pays attention" and "Javier works well with others." My PE teacher said, "Javier is such a polite boy. He even remembers his manners when he is playing basketball and soccer."

Papa will be very happy because he says that right next to a kind heart, a good education is the most important thing we can have. He says that we get our kind hearts by paying attention to the ways of God. We get good educations by working hard at school and trying our best. We must never be lazy, he says.

I always try to do my best because if God exists, and if he is good and fair, I want to have a life that is good and fair, too.

I also want to please my father because I love him. He always tells the truth and does what is right. He works very hard and he wants his children to do good things for the world. I know this because he tells me so at least every week. He says, "Javier, this world is not made for you. You have been made for it. You have been made to do things that bring goodness and peace to a planet that gets weighted down with anger and sadness." Then Papa kisses my cheek and tells me, "Do right, my boy. Be kind, and you will see; the world will be a little different because you are here."

I do not know if I believe all of this yet. I do not know if I even understand it. But I know that I will. Because if Papa says it is true, it must be. So I try and do everything he asks.

But I will tell you a secret before I tell you what I saw today that I should not have seen.

God confuses me.

He really does. Because if there is a god who is good and fair like Papa says, why does genocide happen? If this god is real, why did my brother, Sergio, get killed in the war? I miss my brother very much and I know that my family misses him, too. Even if we do not talk about him.

God could stop genocides and protect soldiers. He could make peace and end wars.

He could if he exists.

But what am I supposed to do if he does exist and these horrible things happen while he is watching? Does this make God evil?

I need to think some more about this. Maybe I will even write some more about it because writing stuff down helps my brain work better. And I know it does not need to work too much better because I already have all A's and I am creative and I work well with others.

But still, writing helps things make sense to me.

And I am telling the truth when I say that I really want to know the truth about God.

But right now I have some questions. So I will believe that there is more to know before I know that I can be serious about believing in God. That is all for now.

I have a stomach ache. I do not know why because I am not hungry and I do not have gas. I know this is true because I ate a half pound burrito from Taco Express that was supposed to be Carmen's two nights ago. It was in the refrigerator for two days so I thought that I better eat it so it would not go to waste.

And after I ate it, my belly did not feel full of bubbles and I have not made any burps. I have not farted either and this is a sign that I do not have gas.

But my belly hurts anyway.

Maybe it hurts because of what Maker and I saw this afternoon.

I will tell what I saw. But since Mr. Steinberg will read this and I will get a grade, I hope he will not be mad. Because Maker and I were not spying. We are not school moles working from the inside. We were only going back to Mr. Steinberg's class so that I could get my jacket before we walked home with Carmen.

It was very cold today. And this is what happened.

Maker met me after school in front of Mrs. Rashani's classroom. Mrs. Rashani teaches third grade and her room is at the end of the hall, right past Maker's fourth grade class and just around the corner from my fifth grade social studies room. Social studies is my last class of the day, so when Carmen sometimes walks me and Maker home, we meet by Mrs. Rashani's room.

So today we met like always. Then Maker dug in his backpack and pulled out his yo-yo. He put his backpack on his shoulders and waited for me to get out my yo-yo. We like to do tricks all the way home.

So I got out my yo-yo and we went outside. Then I remembered that I needed my jacket because it was so cold that my breath would turn the air into white smoke. And Carmen would yell at me if I told her I had to go back and get it.

Inside, the school was pretty empty because almost all the kids were gone. So I told Maker to hurry up and we both started going to Mr. Steinberg's class.

We walked very fast but we were quiet because our shoes do not make squeaky sounds and we did not talk. This is because we were trying to do *Around the World* while we walked fast with our yo-yos.

A minute later, I saw Emma Thompson sitting in front of Mr. Steinberg's classroom. Emma is in my social studies class and she is not a nice girl. She has hair the color of fire that looks like fuzz that you pull out of old carpet. Except hers is long and it all sticks together because I don't think she brushes it.

She also does not brush her teeth. I know this because when she breathes, her mouth smells like Hombre's does after he gets to eat Papa's leftover fish sticks.

I would not care about Emma's bad smell or her crazy hair if she acted nicely.

But she does not.

Instead, Emma makes up lies on the playground and gets even her friends into trouble. She calls people names and she sometimes raises up her skirt and then tells the teacher that some boy in our class is trying to see her underclothes.

I do not like Emma. I think she is dangerous and if Maker and I were ninjas, I think we would just capture her and put her in a room with only Raisin Bran and ginger ale and toilet paper for two weeks.

But today she was not acting dangerous.

She was acting like a big crybaby.

Right in front of Mr. Steinberg's class, Emma was sucking on an apple and crying until shiny clear snot dripped out of her nose. She was not crying very loud, but her face was all wet and full of big pink dots like she had it scrunched up from bawling too long.

Since I was sort of happy to see Emma crying and Maker does not even know the story of Emma's terribleness, we both ignored her and kept walking until we heard someone holler, "Just who do you think you are to be terrifying these children?"

It was a man's voice and it sounded like whoever it was had the body of an ogre. A really big ogre like Shrek. I felt scared and Maker's eyes got as big as a cow's. We both stopped walking. We also quit playing with our yo-yos.

We just stood outside Mr. Steinberg's classroom like we were statues or something. We stood where nobody but Crybaby Emma could see us.

Then we heard Mr. Steinberg answer. He was very calm and quiet. "Mr. Thompson, I understand why you would be concerned."

"Concerned?" The voice that must have been Mr. Thompson's bellowed. "Concerned would be my little Emma hearing about the cholera outbreak in Zimbabwe." I leaned closer to the edge of the door so I could see the screamer. "No, I'm not concerned, Steinberg. I'm downright livid."

Livid means furious and Mr. Thompson definitely was. His face was as red and round as the apple Emma was slobbering on, and his little round glasses shook like they were afraid he might yell at them, too.

"Mr. Thompson, teaching the unit on genocide is new. It's the first time we are doing it, and it's something of a risk. I know that. But when we present history to these kids in a way that's authentic but not too graphic, they connect with the stories they're learning. What's more, they start asking the big questions—questions like why these atrocities happen and what can be done to prevent them in the first place." Mr. Steinberg cleared his throat with two little sounds that he always makes right before he is going to tell us something important. "Sir, I believe that teaching our children about past suffering, about present injustices, may very well be the best way to foster the cultures of action-oriented compassion that our societies so desperately lack and need."

"So you terrify my kid with tales from Auschwitz and horror stories about S-21? *This* is supposed to make her compassionate?"

"Auschwitz and S-21 show us some of the most lurid examples of man's cruelty to man." Mr. Steinberg still sounded patient. "I referred to some of this when I sent home the permission slip for the children to attend the Holocaust Museum. On that same sheet, I also explained that if we don't talk about these things, if we don't explain history's darkest lessons to this generation, the mistakes that have continued to allow genocide or other crimes against humanity will only continue."

I felt really proud of Mr. Steinberg even though I did not understand a few of the words he used. But I agreed with him and I would have liked to tell Mr. Thompson so.

Kids understand more than some adults think that we do. We are not stupid and our brains are not filled with marshmallows. We understand stuff if smart older people like Mr. Steinberg just explain things using words and ideas that make sense to us. And then we feel proud of ourselves for being young but very smart.

"My little Emma has been terribly upset about these...these... genocides," Mr. Thompson boomed again. "She says they're hard on her. They upset her."

"Mr. Thompson, whether or not we realize it, genocide is hard on everyone. But please remember this: It's hardest on those who are living through such violence. It's most devastating to those people who have no way of protecting themselves or securing peace for their people or country." I saw part of Mr. Steinberg sit on his desk because Maker and I were peeking around the door where we could only see about half of everything in the front of the classroom. "I assure you, Emma may be saddened and somewhat disturbed by this history, but I'm teaching nothing that will terrify any student. I'm giving basic insight into six major genocides of the twentieth century."

"So basic insight is talking about the Warsaw Ghetto and death marches and assassinations on the streets of Constantinople? You call this basic insight?"

Mr. Steinberg was quiet for a long time.

"Sir, please tell me, what are you objecting to? What exactly do you not want Emma to learn?"

Mr. Thompson stepped closer to Mr. Steinberg and stuck his big red face very close to my teacher's.

"Bottom line, Steinberg? I object to all of this. To this whole unit or whatever you want to call it. Genocide is not for children."

"Genocide, Mr. Thompson, should not be for anyone. Intentionally destroying a race of people should not be something any human being would ever have to encounter. But keeping those who could or would help ignorant of these crimes is wrong because..."

"Don't preach to me about right and wrong, Steinberg. You're already on thin ice because I'm taking this to the board next month..."

"Please feel free to do so. It's well within your rights and I thank God that we live in a country where we can have these conversations. I'm thankful we have a system of checks and balances that keep us answering to each other."

"Don't give me the mumbo jumbo godspeak." Mr. Thompson was breathing really hard as he plopped into one of our little class chairs and pulled it close to the desk where Mr. Steinberg still sat. He is a very big man so the chair sort of groaned and squealed as he dragged it. "Not all of us choose to answer to the idea of a god. Some of us do not want God or faith or anything like it forced on us or on our children. And in the public school system..."

I watched Mr. Steinberg stand up. Now he did not look quite as patient. He did not look like a social studies teacher.

He looked a little bit like a soldier and a little like a king. I know about soldiers and kings because my brother was a soldier before he was killed. And Aragorn was the best king ever in my *Lord of the Rings* books.

"Michael, I am well aware of what I can and cannot teach children. I am entirely apprised of how matters of faith need to be handled in the classroom." Mr. Steinberg took a deep breath. "And yes, I do have a personal faith. I ascribe to a being greater than me and hope that I live my life accordingly. But this is not something I discuss with these children. And it's certainly not part of this conversation."

Mr. Thompson looked all snarky. I love the word snarky. It means all smart-alecky and sarcastic. I learned this word from Liliana. She says Carmen is snarky.

"You're almost right, Steinberg. God should not be part of this conversation. But *you* introduced him. *You* assigned possibility to the idea. And now I'm starting to think that maybe you're teaching these kids this...this...terror in the classroom out of your sense of morality or duty to some faith."

I watched my teacher carefully to see what he would do. Mr. Thompson was not being kind and he was not being fair. So I wanted to see what would happen next. And for one second, I really wanted for Maker and me to be ninjas so we could make this right. But I looked at Maker's face and I decided that he might not be a good ninja because he looked very scared and not powerful the way ninjas need to be.

"I am teaching this class about genocide because I, along with our principal, Mr. Tate, and the school board, believe that in order for our society to care about human issues and human rights, we need to first understand them. We need to be informed about those things that are wrong, those systems that are broken. Then we need to be taught that every one of us can and should make a difference." Mr. Steinberg looked like he meant serious business.

"That's ignorant. Downright ignorant. A bunch of kids getting terrified about past mass killings around the globe cannot possibly make any kind of difference. Except that they'll have nightmares and wind up in psychiatric care for the anxiety disorders they develop from this. That's the only kind of difference that'll happen." Mr. Thompson stood up and breathed out really hard. I saw Mr. Steinberg pull back a little. I wondered if he did this because Mr. Thompson's breath smelled fishy the same way Emma's does. "You're an idiot, Eliot Steinberg. An idiot with no family of your own. So you start filling up these kids' heads with stuff that you have no idea about except from the history books you pore over while you're all alone, holed up in your crummy little apartment somewhere."

"Mr. Thompson, we can certainly disagree. It's obvious that we do. But attacking my personal life and calling me names will accomplish nothing. Perhaps it's best that you take up your concerns with Mr. Tate and the school board."

Right then, something really incredible happened.

Before Mr. Thompson could say anything else, Maker's father, Jengmer Jok, was in the classroom. Just like that. Suddenly he was standing next to Mr. Steinberg like he had appeared from nowhere. Only I knew that he had come from somewhere – and that somewhere had been from the back door of our classroom on the other side of the hall.

I looked at Maker. His eyes were even bigger and rounder than before. I could tell that he was as surprised as I was.

"Hello, Jengmer." Mr. Steinberg extended his hand to Mr. Jok. Then he made a nod at Mr. Thompson. "This is Mr. Michael Thompson, the father of a student in my class."

Mr. Jok only stared at Mr. Thompson. He did not smile. He did not put out his hand the way I have seen him do when he says hello to people. He just stared and looked like a very tall and fierce warrior. He looked like a powerful African chief. Except that he had on fancy business clothes that I have never seen him wearing before. And I thought that if he switched out those clothes, he would make a very fine ninja if I ever needed an extra one. In fact, I might even ask him to be in charge of my ninja web if I decide to have one.

"Jengmer, I'm finishing up with Mr. Thompson, so I'll be with you in just a minute. Please feel free to go into the teacher's lounge and have some refreshments. Lunch was brought in earlier and I think there are a few sandwiches left in the fridge."

I wondered why Mr. Jok would be invited into the teacher's lounge and I wondered what he was doing in that room in the first place. Maker is only in the fourth grade so he does not have Mr. Steinberg for his teacher.

So how does Mr. Jok know my teacher? And what was he doing in my classroom?

I could tell Maker also had questions in his mind. And I could tell that he was afraid that his father would see us spying if we were not careful. If Mr. Jok came out the front door of our class instead of going back out like he came in, we were busted. Besides, Crybaby Emma was still making loud sniffs and lapping on that apple. Mr. Jok might think that Maker and me were the ones who made that evil girl start bawling in the first place.

Maker looked like he had to go to the bathroom but I knew it was not because he had to *go*. It was because Mr. Jok was about to come out of that room one way or the other.

Mr. Jok just stared some more at Mr. Thompson. It was not a very nice stare. Then he turned around and started walking to the back of the classroom. He was going out like he came in and I felt warm air on my neck from Maker's big sigh.

Mr. Jok is a giant. He is as tall as Luol Deng of the Chicago Bulls. His skin is the same amazing color as Luol Deng's, too.

The color of midnight in the country when almost no stars are out.

I know about midnight in the country because I went to the country once with my friend, Steven Pappadopolis. But this was before he moved to Texas.

So Mr. Jok was gone. Now it was just Mr. Steinberg and Mr. Thompson alone in that classroom. And Emma hiccupping and slurping on her apple. She was not blubbering anymore, and for the first time, I wondered what she had been bawling about.

Probably to get someone in trouble.

Probably Mr. Steinberg.

I gave Emma a mean look. But not too mean because I was scared that she would start that crybaby stuff and my teacher and Mr. Thompson would hurry out into the hall.

Then Maker and I would be busted. We would be sent to see Mr. Tate for spying.

So Maker and I both pressed ourselves real tight against the wall and peeked back into the classroom. Mr. Steinberg had walked behind his desk and he was acting busy by putting papers into little stacks. Mr. Thompson just stood with his hands in his pockets. His belly flopped over his belt and from where I stood, it looked like he had two rumps.

A rump is really a behind, but I do not like this word, and Papa says I cannot say "butt." But Mr. Thompson looks like he has two of them (rumps, I mean). A real one in back and a belly-rump out front.

"Thank you for your concern, Mr. Thompson. I need to be going now. Please do feel free to talk with Mr. Tate."

"I'll go now, Steinberg. But this isn't over. This school had no business hiring an old guy like you to teach kids. You're way out of touch, and what you know about genocide or anything like it comes from dusty history books." Mr. Thompson gave a big old sniff like a dog does. "You need to let the past stay in the past. And maybe it'd be good if you just thought about getting out of here."

"Mr. Thompson, you cannot possibly know what my experience with this topic is. And though you may get your wish and find me gone at some point in the near future, you're wrong about genocide being something belonging to only the past."

"What on earth are you concocting now?"

"Genocide, acts of genocide, crimes against humanity. They're all alive and well. Go home and see for yourself. Google Darfur. Investigate what's happening in the Democratic Republic of the Congo. And don't forget: Southern Sudan and Rwanda weren't too long ago."

"What's your point?"

My teacher sighed. "History repeats itself. The past becomes the present with all of its pains and mistakes. Unless we interrupt cycles of injustice before they wind up being the future that our kids inherit."

"Since you have no kids, Steinberg, you don't need to worry about what they inherit or not..."

"Mr. Thompson, that will be enough now. We have finished this conversation."

Mr. Thompson got real quiet. For a minute, he just stood in front of Mr. Steinberg's desk and watched my teacher pack up his stuff into an old briefcase. Then he said this:

"Just tell me one thing, Steinberg. Why teach this to our kids? And what's it all to you?"

Mr. Steinberg stopped packing up his things. He tugged at his beard and looked straight at Mr. Thompson.

"Because children haven't gotten jaded or apathetic yet. They're not too busy or distracted to care. They want the world to be a better place and they believe that they can help make it so. And as far as what this topic means to me, that, Mr. Thompson, is something you would never understand. Not even if you somehow managed to get as old as I am."

Then they both started walking so Maker and I had to get away. We had to make a break for it which was not hard because our shoes are the same kind, and like I said, they do not squeak. So I gave Emma my most "you're history if you even make one little noise" look and then we sprinted away. I know about sprinting because I sometimes watch the Sports Channel with Papa.

So now I am home. I am in my room and I have looked up apathetic and jaded in the dictionary. *Jaded* means worn out, with a sometimes-attitude and *apathetic* means that you don't really care about something.

Mr. Steinberg is right. Kids are not usually jaded because adults take care of us and make us get enough food and sleep and our homework all finished. And we are not apathetic because most of us like to care about stuff. We are good at caring about things.

So we are good people to tell about genocide.

But I will tell Papa about everything that I saw because if you ask me, Mr. Thompson was being horrible to my teacher. And since I was not spying, Papa will understand and he will explain to me some more about what I saw.

I already know this, though: Genocide is a tricky thing to talk about. It sounds like it is tricky when that UN tries to work stuff out about helping in countries where big killings are happening. It was tricky for Raphael Lemkin and tricky for some of the people who tried to help make things better in Armenia and Cambodia and during the Holocaust.

But it is even tricky when plain people like Mr. Steinberg try to do the right thing and tell plain kids like the fifth graders at Roosevelt Elementary about race killing.

I just think that some people do not want to hear about it.

Maybe they do not want to hear because then they will know that bad things are happening. And then they will have to decide whether they will just be a watcher or whether they will be brave and become a doer.

Maybe I am wrong, but it seems like if you know that horrible things are happening to a group of people, you should do something about it.

Like Mr. Steinberg said, we should do the thing that we can do.

Even if we do not know the people. Even if those people do not look like us or believe the same things we do.

We should still care enough to get brave and do and say stuff that sticks up for them.

I know that if bad governments and mean people were doing race killing here in America, I would want people far away to care about helping me. Besides, in the way that my Papa and Mama think, you treat people exactly like you want to be treated.

Since I like to be remembered and I like it when people are good to me, I think that I know something true.

I have some work to do. Some work that helps make genocides go away.

And I have to do it even if it gets tricky.

P.S. I need to tell the truth about how I wrote all of this. I know it says December 1 as the date for all of this stuff. But it really took me two days to write this much. It took me this long because I had a lot to write and my hand gets tired. So I took many little breaks and wrote when I wanted to.

CHAPTER 12

HELLO J,

Today is Wednesday again and Maker will come over in a little while. Tonight we get to eat a pizza of our own. This is happening because Lili is studying for those big tests and Carmen has to be in her room every day for one week. Right after school she has to come straight to our apartment and go right into her room. This is because Papa heard her saying some words in Spanish that he said were full of attitude.

I am glad Carmen is in her room for two reasons. The first reason is I do not have to see her and this is fine with me. The second reason is I like pizza, and if Carmen had to cook because Liliana is busy, I would be eating beans and slimy hot dogs with Maker tonight.

I think Maker and I will choose pepperoni pizza with extra cheese. I also think that if I ask nicely, Papa or Lili will let us have a can of root beer each from the refrigerator.

I am very excited about this. But I am acting extra normal. This is because I am eleven now and I have to be grown up about things like catching frogs and getting pizza and missing my Mama.

So here is my new idea (I am not talking about pizza anymore; now I am thinking about genocide): I might have to rip out some of these pages in this journal.

I might have to tear them out because they know too much. They know too much because I have written stuff down on them about Mr. Steinberg and Mr. Thompson and stinky Crybaby Emma. Maybe I should not have written these things.

So I will have to decide what I think I should do later.

I mean, I want to keep these pages in this book because they tell the truth about what I am learning. But I saw something that I should not have the other day.

And I do not want to be blamed for being a spy.

So I might keep these pages from the other day and today. And I might not.

I told Papa about what Maker and I saw after school. I knew he would believe that I was telling the truth and not trying to be a spy or anything.

I was right. He did not get mad at me at all. He just rubbed his chin and made some noises in his throat while I explained. Then he asked me two or three questions that I do not remember now.

He also asked me how I felt about things.

I told him that I felt bad about genocide. I told him that I want to do some things that help stop it or keep it from starting in the first place.

Then I said that I felt especially terrible about Mr. Steinberg because all he is trying to do is help kids learn to do the right thing. And instead of getting respect and nice treatment for his hard work, he gets Mr. Thompson being all mean to him.

Papa said that sometimes doing a good or right thing has a big cost. He said that people sometimes have a hard time when something new happens and the new thing changes the way that things have been in the past.

In the past, not too many elementary school kids like me have learned about genocide. We have not learned about what it is and why it happens and how we can help make it go away. Usually, much older kids like Carmen learn about it. And even then, Papa said that not very much is taught to the older students.

Mr. Steinberg is trying out something new. He is teaching fifth graders about a very hard subject. He is teaching them a lot, and then he will show them how they can do some things that might help.

Papa says that this is noble work. *Noble* means very good in a brave and strong way.

But not everyone likes the kind of thing that my teacher is doing. And Mr. Thompson disliked this genocide teaching so much that he used very mean words when he talked to my teacher.

Papa said that it sounded like Mr. Steinberg had been kind and fair even though Emma's father had not been. Papa said that in times when people are not being kind and fair to us, it is even more important for us to behave like my teacher had. He said that a person's character shows itself the most when that person is put under pressure or not treated fairly. **After all, anybody can be nice to people who are nice to them**. This is easy.

So I guess Mr. Steinberg has good character.

I think that I might have some good character, too, because I put up with Carmen's food and her burps. I do not yell back at her even if she screams at me, and I never pull Emma Thompson's hair or tell her that she has breath like Hombre's after he eats fish sticks.

I might even be noble. But I am not sure about this.

What I am sure about is I will start doing some work about genocide.

Today Mr. Steinberg told us some ways we can help.

These are some of the ways:

Students like me can write to some of our government leaders who are helping make laws in America. These leaders are the ones that we choose by voting for them. When they get picked, they are called our *elected officials.*

The best elected official to write to is probably our congressperson in the U.S. House of Representatives. Every state has some of these members of Congress who act for the people living in the districts that they work for. *District* just means a certain area where something is.

So we can write to our members of Congress and say that we want genocide to stop when we know that it is happening. We can also send e-mails or make phone calls to their offices. Sometimes, we can even get people together and make visits to their offices! But first, we have to ask our parents if this is okay to do (besides, we would need for them to help us with a lot of this).

We can also write, e-mail or call our senators. Every state has two U.S. senators and all together, these senators make up the United States Senate (the U.S. House of Representatives plus the U.S. Senate make up the United States Congress). Writing or calling or e-mailing these senators and telling them that we want genocide to stop can be helpful. And when there are some new ideas for laws that would help genocide stop, we can tell our U.S. senators and our other members of Congress that we want them to get in there and work to make sure those ideas get turned into laws!

Since our congresspersons and our senators work for the people in their districts and states, they have to listen to our ideas. So when we have ideas and plans about stopping and preventing genocide, we can talk with them.

Another way that we can be doers and not just watchers is we can find some groups that work to stop genocide and keep it from happening in the first place. When we keep something from happening in the first place, it is called *preventing*. We can ask our papas and mamas to go online with us and find these groups that are doing this kind of work. Then we can read about what they do and how we can help them. Mr. Steinberg said that the Enough Project (www.enoughproject.org) and Genocide Intervention Network (www.genocideintervention.net) are just a couple of the very good groups that do this here in D.C.

These groups can often use donations to keep doing their work. My teacher said that efforts that help stop and prevent genocide cannot happen for free. So we can give some of our money if our parents say this is okay.

Sometimes the groups ask people who care about genocide to get together and do things in their communities that will tell others about a genocide that is happening. These gatherings where this happens are called *rallies* or *vigils*. And during these gatherings, new people learn about genocide from other people who already know and care about it. The new people get to learn ways that they can take action and be doers, too!

Mr. Steinberg also said that religious groups have done incredible things to help end human suffering. He said that through the ages, people of faith have worked very hard to stop injustices and bring about good and fair treatment of mistreated people. He told us about men like Olaudah Equiano, Frederick Douglass, William Wilberforce and Mahatma Gandhi. He told us about women like Harriett Beecher Stowe and Harriett Tubman and Rosa Parks and Mother Teresa.

People of faith, Mr. Steinberg said, are some of the greatest resources we can have in the work of trying to end

genocide. This is because they are often very serious about following teachings that require them to care about others—especially those who cannot defend themselves. So he said that getting leaders in our churches or synagogues or mosques involved is a very fine idea.

Another thing Mr. Steinberg told us about is doing projects that make some money while they tell others that genocide is happening. For an example, me and Maker could make some chocolate chip cookies on Saturday and sell them to the people in our apartment complex. We could also make some flyers that tell what is happening in that part of Sudan called Darfur. And we could leave the flyers with the cookies that the people buy.

But instead of keeping the money, we could give some of it to a group that is working to help make genocides stop. Then we could give the rest of the money to a group that is helping people in places where genocide is happening. These groups that help the suffering people are called *humanitarian aid organizations.* This is just a big name that means groups that are helping people get things like food, water, clothes and medicine. And Mr. Steinberg said that there are a lot of these groups besides some very big helping organizations that are part of the United Nations.

All of these groups would probably appreciate some extra money to keep helping the people who are hurt by genocide.

There are some other things that we can do to help, but this is all Mr. Steinberg told us about today. He said that soon we would be studying the genocides in Bosnia and Rwanda and Sudan. Bosnia is in Europe and Rwanda and Sudan are in Africa.

Oh, one more thing before I quit writing: Our teacher said that last year something called the Genocide Prevention Task Force (a *task force* just means a team of people working on a special job) was created to help our country pay attention to helping prevent genocide. The work of this team is also to come up with suggestions that help our government take action when there are signs and threats of genocide. The groups that got this task force together are the U.S. Holocaust Memorial Museum, the American Academy of Diplomacy and the United States Institute of Peace. Mr. Steinberg said that very soon the Genocide Prevention Task Force will be sending out a report that gives advice and ideas to help our country help prevent genocide. He said this team is led by two people who have had very important jobs in the United States government: former Secretary of State Madeleine Albright and former Secretary of Defense William Cohen. I think that this team is a very good idea.

So now I will stop writing. But first, I have to say that Mr. Steinberg seemed very sad and tired today. He seemed like his mind had gray clouds all around it and that he wanted to go home. He said that we would be finished learning about genocide by our winter holidays.

I wonder if he is glad. I wonder if he is sorry that he has started teaching us about this subject that is causing hard times for him. I also wonder about Mr. Jok and him. I wonder about why Mr. Steinberg would know Mr. Jok enough to tell him to eat sandwiches in the teacher's lounge. The teacher's lounge is a very important place. I also am thinking about the fancy clothes Mr. Jok was wearing on Monday.

I know that this is a lot of questions. But they are in my head and it feels good to write them down. Especially since I do not know if I will keep these papers in my journal.

CHAPTER 13

HELLO BOOK ABOUT GENOCIDE,

Today I will write about God. I will do this because Mr. Steinberg told our class some more reasons why genocide happens. Fights about God is a reason.

He said that genocide is complicated and that many things go into it happening. He said it was a little like making a cake.

When you make a cake, you have to have certain things in it for it to become a cake. You have to put in flour. You have to add sugar and stuff that makes the cake get puffy. There has to be eggs in most cakes and butter or oil.

Then you have to put it in a pan and cook it at the right kind of temperature. If you do all of this, you get a nice cake to eat.

Well, getting a genocide is not nice at all. But like cakes, certain ingredients have to get mixed together for genocides to happen.

Mr. Steinberg said that one of the ingredients of race killing has to do with some big stresses between the groups of people that live in the places where the genocide happens. Kind of like the Turks and the Armenians. And the Jewish people and German Nazis.

What often happens is the group that has power might not like another group (or groups) of people that live in the same country. So the group in power starts picking on the other group or groups. Then they keep getting meaner and meaner.

And sometimes this cruel treatment turns into hurting and killing those people of a group that the leaders with power do not like.

These angry and unfair leaders might not like people who are different from them. They might not like people with different colored skin or people who speak another language and believe differently than they do.

So they make a plan to get rid of those who are different than themselves.

Another reason that some leaders in governments hurt the people in their countries is because of something called natural resources. I know about natural resources because of my science class. *Natural resources* are things that come out of the earth that we use to make stuff or help serve other people with. Some natural resources are trees and minerals and soil and water and oil. Trees get turned into wood and paper and other stuff. Minerals get used to make cell phones and BlackBerrys® and iPods™ - and other minerals are expensive jewels like diamonds and gold. Here are some of the minerals that Mr. Steinberg told us to copy off of the board:

Tin	Tantalum	Copper
Tungsten	Coltan	Uranium
Cassiterite	Diamonds	Cobalt
Rubies	Gold	Manganese

He said that there are a whole bunch more. This is just some. And what happens is people all over the world want or need these minerals. But the sad thing is these minerals are often in countries where there are already some struggles going on. The struggles are often between groups of people and sometimes between the people and the government that is in charge.

So big fights happen over who will get to the natural resources first. The group that gets them will sell the minerals to people and companies that will pay a lot of money for them. These companies and people that buy the natural resources really want these minerals. They want them so that they can make stuff like computers and cell phones and DVD players (and other things). Once these things are made, they get sold to people in countries around the world.

So terrible fighting and killing happens because everybody wants these resources so that they can make money.

Mr. Steinberg said that it is important to remember that many lands that have a lot of natural resources also have very poor people living in them. Many of the people who live in these places have less than one or two dollars a day to take care of themselves and their families. This is very poor.

So these poor people will fight other groups of people for the resources. This is especially true when the resources are on the very land where they live!

This makes sense, if you ask me. Because if the resources are in the same place where the people are living, it would be normal for those people to feel like the minerals belong to them. But other groups, and sometimes government leaders, say that they should get the resources.

So it all gets to be very horrible and millions of people have died—and keep dying—because of fighting about diamonds and gold and oil and other natural resources.

Mr. Steinberg said that the natural resources do not cause genocide, exactly. He said that stuff like oil and diamonds cannot make race killing happen.

But when people disagree over these resources that could make lots of money, big fights over them break out. Then the killings start. Mr. Steinberg said that this had happened for many years in southern Sudan.

He said that there is a lot of oil in southern Sudan.

The government leaders in the north part of Sudan knew about this oil. And they wanted it because when oil gets taken out of the earth (this is called *extraction*), it can be sold to companies that will buy it. Then these companies sell and use the oil in other parts of the world.

So the northern leaders in Sudan made some business deals with some companies around the world. They made agreements that would take the oil out of the south part of Sudan. Then the oil would get moved from southern Sudan to northern Sudan by putting in a pipeline.

China put in the pipeline that carries the oil from the south to the north.

But there was a big problem: There were villages of different tribes of people that lived on the same land where the oil was.

So the government of Sudan began to do terrible things to get the people off of the land. They did this so that they could get to the oil.

Northern Sudanese leaders sent in soldiers on camels and horses to go in and kill the people. They did some of this killing by shooting the tribal people with guns.

They did this by buying planes from countries like Russia and then using the planes to drop bombs onto the villages of the people.

Sudanese government soldiers also set big fires to whole villages. This made the villages burn up.

There is more to tell about Sudan, Mr. Steinberg said. He said that he had gotten things out of order by telling us about oil in Sudan. But this is because he was teaching us some reasons genocide happens.

And one of those reasons has to do with big fights over the natural resources in lands where people are already stressed and prejudiced about some differences.

Another big reason genocide happens is because of impunity. I have already talked some about this, but *impunity* means that no punishments or consequences happen when wrong things get done to people or places. And Mr. Steinberg said that if bad leaders do not get stopped from hurting or killing groups that are different (and sometimes weaker) than them, they will keep it up. They will keep it up because they know that nobody will stop them. So they can just do what they want.

What is even more terrible is this: When other leaders see that past governments like those in Armenia and Germany and Cambodia got away with big race killings, they know that they might get away with it, too.

So they get brave in this horrible way.

And they start genocides in their own countries.

Now I will stop writing for a little while because I need to use the bathroom and feed Hombre before Maker comes. He is coming again tonight which is good because we did not have our pizza or root beer last night. I am very hungry and I think that Maker will be hungry, too. So I will wash my hands and face in the bathroom when I am all done going. I will even comb my hair because Papa says that being clean and having manners is important.

Then I will ask for a large pepperoni pizza with extra cheese instead of a medium one. And because I am all fresh and polite, I think that Papa will say yes to me and then let me and Maker have a root beer each from the refrigerator.

But I will come back later tonight and talk about God and religion. I wanted to do this first.

Instead, I got carried away telling you other stuff.

I will tell you this though: Fighting about God is also one of the reasons genocides happen.

* * *

Now I am back. Maker just went home with Mr. Jok, who was dressed in some more fancy clothes. I do not understand these clothes because I thought that Maker's father was a security guard in one of the big buildings close to where my Papa works. He usually wears these dark blue and gray guard clothes and he almost always carries a lot of books with him.

Now he looks like a tall African chief in business clothes.

I think that this is weird, but since I am polite and maybe noble, I am being quiet and not saying anything. Except to Hombre.

Maker and I got to have our large pizza and our root beer. Then for a surprise, Papa made us sopapillas and let us put as much honey as we wanted on them. I ate four pieces of pizza and three sopapillas so my stomach feels very full.

Now I will you tell you about another reason for genocide and that reason is fights about God. Mr. Steinberg said that throughout history, groups of people have killed each other because one group might think one way about God and another group thinks a different way. He said that we saw this with Armenia and Cambodia—and even with the Holocaust.

During the Holocaust, whatever Hitler thought about God was different than what the Jewish people believed about God. With Armenia, there were different ideas between what the Armenian Christians believed from what the Muslim Young Turks did. And in Cambodia, the Buddhist monks and Cham Muslim people had different religious beliefs than Communism. Communism does not let people believe in a god because the leaders in Communist countries think that religion gets in the way of people doing what the leaders want them to do.

Mr. Steinberg said that we would see more about how religion is one of the reasons genocide happens. **But he said that religion all by itself does not really cause genocide. He said**

that it is when leaders use their different beliefs about faith to get power over other groups that dangerous fighting can start. People like to be free to believe the way that they choose. So when one group of people tries to force their ideas about faith on another group that has different ideas, terrible things can happen.

So I guess like my teacher said, a lot of things make up why genocides start. I guess if you mix up things like stress and prejudice between different tribes or groups of people and fights about natural resources—plus that thing called impunity—you could have very big problems. But then if you also have some of the very poorest people in the world all worried about trying to take care of their families and then some more fights about religion...well, I can see how genocide happens.

And how it is like a cake with disgusting, horrible, terrible ingredients.

Mr. Steinberg said that we could remember that genocide happens when all of the right "wrong" conditions for it exist in a place.

Cody Bracewell asked our teacher how come big fights about religion and God did not happen in America. He said that he has friends who have very different ideas about God. But they all get along very nicely.

Mr. Steinberg said that people in the United States do have different ideas about God and faith. He said that some people believe in God. Others do not. And those who do believe often have very different ideas from other people who believe.

But in America, people have the freedom to think and believe as they please. People can choose to believe in God the way that they wish. For those who do not want to believe in a god, they are also free to have this idea.

Mr. Steinberg said that religious freedom is one of the rights of people who live in our country. He also said that our government is set up to stay out of the business of religion. And religion does not take part in government. The two things of religion and government are separated and this is called *separation of church and state.*

I think that our government is very smart. Mr. Steinberg said that the men who made up the ways that our country is organized were brilliant. America is organized by what the

United States Constitution says, and the men who thought the Constitution up are called the *framers* of it. They did this more than two hundred years ago and I think that even though they had funny hair and weird clothes, these framers were the smartest men ever.

Now I will go to sleep. I am tired and I will not brush my teeth because Liliana fell asleep on the couch with her big fat book and Carmen does not care what I do. I think Carmen is burping right now because Lili is not in the room with her and Papa went to sleep one hour ago.

I know that I am a boy and that I am supposed to think that burps are cool. But I do not like the sound or the smells of burps.

That is all now. But I am sorry about all of these reasons for genocide and I am the most sorry about the one where people get in fights about God.

Because if God is good and fair, I do not think that he would want people having fights about him.

And I really do not think he would like it if people kill people and then say it was because of what they thought about him.

CHAPTER 14

DEAR JOURNAL,

I cannot write today. I cannot write because I am very upset. Lili says that when a person is supposed to write something but they cannot think of words, this is called writer's block.

I think that I am a writer because I write a lot and I do it even when I do not have to. And I am blocked because I cannot make thoughts come into my head.

So I will write only this: Today Mr. Thompson came back after school. I know about this because I saw him and heard some more bad things.

I promise that I was not being a spy or anything. I just forgot my math book in Mr. Steinberg's class. I was almost home when I remembered it, and Carmen yelled at me the whole way back to school.

When we got there, I went inside to get my book and there was that old bully-man. Yelling at my teacher. But this time, Emma was not with him and Mr. Thompson was even more mean.

He told my teacher that teaching about genocide was a stupid thing to do.

He told him that he knew nothing about children or what it was like to have a family.

And then he told Mr. Steinberg that the best thing that could happen to this school was for him to go to a place where genocide is happening—and never, ever come back.

CHAPTER 15

J,

Here is a weird thing: Mr. Steinberg did not come to school today.

That is not the weird part because sometimes even teachers get diseases and have to stay home and blow their noses. They probably have to drink soup and cough medicine and see the doctor if their disease gets really bad.

I hardly ever have to see the doctor because I am robust and swarthy. Papa says so and he learned the words from his book that helps him get a better vocabulary. But since *swarthy* means something about having darker skin like the color of caramel or chocolate instead of like vanilla ice cream, I do not think that my swarthiness has anything to do with me not having to see the doctor.

Just my robustness does.

Anyway, I know that Mr. Steinberg did not have any diseases today because our principal, Mr. Tate, came into our class and told us so.

This is what he said:

Mr. Steinberg will not be in class for an indeterminate period of time. When Rusty White asked what that big word meant, our principal said *indeterminate* meant that we did not know when Mr. Steinberg would be returning. He said that Mr. Steinberg had some serious things he had to take care of.

I thought that maybe his new kitten, Loko Bai, died or something like that. My teacher just got this cat a few weeks after school started. But Mr. Tate said that Mr. Steinberg's absence in our class had nothing to do with Loko Bai.

He said that we would have a very able substitute teacher to finish telling our class about the three more genocides we need to study. I did not ask Mr. Tate what he meant about the substitute being *able*, but I thought that sounded really silly. Because a person would have to be able to do something if he or she was going to do it. Otherwise they would be *unable*, and all of this made no sense to me. But I just stayed still and quiet in my seat so Mr. Tate would keep thinking to himself that I am very polite and intelligent.

Then Mr. Tate said that we could write in our journals for the rest of the class if we wanted. But we had to mind Mrs. Rashani, who would be keeping an eye on us since she had a student teacher in her classroom watching her third graders.

That was all he said except that the new substitute teacher would be in our class tomorrow. And his name is Dr. Jengmer Jok.

I know a Jengmer Jok. This is the name of Maker's papa.

But Maker's papa is not a doctor who makes diseases go away. He is not an able substitute teacher for fifth grade social studies students.

He is just a plain man who guards big buildings and likes books and plays chess even better than Maker.

So Mr. Tate must be talking about another man named Jengmer Jok.

CHAPTER 16

DEAR J,

Are you ready for some more weirdness? Maker's papa is our substitute teacher!

I think this is crazy because Mr. Jok cannot be a doctor. He works in big buildings. Not in classrooms. And he never wears white cardboard shirts and movie star pants. I know about his clothes because until one or two weeks ago, I would always see him in his uniform.

When he came into our room today, he acted all normal with me. He smiled and told me that it was nice to see me and that Maker said that I was getting so good at chess that I would be beating him soon.

So I know that this man is not an imposter. He is really Mr. Jok. Besides, he even smelled like Mr. Jok, and this is a smell of soap and hair oil and something else that is spicy.

But Mr. Jok did not explain anything to me. He did not tell me why he was not in his uniform or why he was standing here in my fifth grade social studies class. He just wrote his name on the board while all of the other kids came into our room and sat in their seats.

None of them were surprised to see *Dr. Jok* written in neat letters on our chalkboard.

If Mr. Jok is really Dr. Jok, I wondered why he was not wearing a doctor's coat instead of his fancy business clothes. But I did not have to wonder about this too long because Ahmed Naghavi asked him where his doctor coat was. Ahmed knows about doctor coats because his father wears one when he operates on sick people at the hospital where he works.

Mr. Jok smiled at all of us and gave a little bow. He said that he was glad to be our teacher while Mr. Steinberg was absent and that he would do his best to answer as many of our questions as possible.

He explained that he was not a doctor who made sick people well. He was a doctor because he had studied a certain subject for many years and gone to many schools to learn and become like an expert.

When he said that, I hoped that he would be an expert in explaining the rest of the genocides to our class. I also wondered about the places where Mr. Dr. Jok had gone to school. I did not know about any of these places. I only know that he comes from Sudan and that he wears his guard uniform a lot and that he reads even more books than me (which is a lot of books).

But I did not say any of this to the people in my class. I just thought it to myself. I decided that maybe I might ask Mr. Dr. Jok some questions the next time that I go to Maker's apartment.

But what I really want to know is where is my teacher, and how and why does he know my best friend's father, who is also a doctor besides being a plain, tall guy who works in big buildings.

I am not just a little bit confused.

It is lucky for Maker's father that I am now eleven years old. This is lucky for him because even though I am confused, I am very grown up. And this means that I can hold my questions back the same way I do not act too happy about having pizza or being glad that Carmen has to stay in her room.

When you get to be eleven, you definitely get to be cool about things. I know because I am cool even though my hair still sticks up and my belly is sort of like a marshmallow after you put it in the microwave for nine seconds.

Anyway, Mr. Dr. Jok said that we had to learn about three more genocides by the end of next week. If you ask me, this is a lot of genocides to talk about, and unless our substitute teacher really knows about these things, it will not happen.

Because genocide is complicated.

And talking about three of them very quickly and right before Christmas would be hard for even Mr. Steinberg.

But Mr. Dr. Jok said for all of us to get out some paper so we could take notes to write in our journals later. He said that it was time to talk about the genocide that happened in Bosnia and Herzegovina.

Bosnia and Herzegovina (together they are called BiH, which is fine with me because the other names hurt to write if I do it too much) is a heart-shaped land in southeast Europe. It has mountains—in fact, the Dinaric Alps go through there—and hills and a lot of rivers and streams and forests. BiH is now surrounded by the countries of Croatia, Serbia and Montenegro.

This country is really beautiful and I think it would be a great place to see in person. I know that it is very pretty because Mr. Dr. Jok showed us pictures.

But starting in 1991, some horrible things happened there. These awful things had to do with some fights between three groups of people that lived around each other—the Serbs (these are people of Eastern Orthodox religion), the Croats (these people are mostly of the Catholic religion) and the Bosnian Muslims (Muslim people are followers of the religion Islam).

Here is a little more about how all of the bad stuff got to happen.

A long time ago—after the First World War—the country of Yugoslavia got created. The country was made up of different cultural and religious groups (but mostly Croats, Serbs and Muslims). And they all got put into the same country even though they had had disagreements among themselves.

But during World War II, Hitler's German forces invaded Yugoslavia and the country got all divided up, sort of like you cut up a pie or something. Then after Germany got defeated, a strong Communist leader named Josip Broz Tito came along and got the country to hold together. But when he died in 1980, Yugoslavia had some serious problems. Then it got worse in 1987 when a new Serb leader, Slobodan Milosevic became in charge.

All of the old troubles about religion and culture differences got stirred up and fights started happening. This definitely happened in the province of Kosovo. A *province* is an area or territory that is usually within a country or a state.

So the little countries that made up Yugoslavia began to say that they would separate from the country of Yugoslavia. They would be *independent*—or in charge of themselves. Slovenia and Croatia did this in 1991.

Well, the Serb people (a lot of them were from the Republic of Serbia, but Serbs lived in other republics, too) did not like this at all. They wanted a bigger Serbia, and they did not want Yugoslavia to just break up into little independent countries. So Milosevic sent in Serbian troops (since he was in charge of the country's powerful military) to try and stop Slovenia and Croatia from breaking away. This army did a lot of damage, especially in Croatia. There, the Serbian soldiers fought and killed the Croat people for eighty-six days in the city of Vukovar. But Croatia still got to be independent and so did Slovenia.

The world did not do too much to stop all of this. Many government leaders said that this was a war between the people in Yugoslavia, which is a civil war. In *civil wars*, where people in a country fight each other, other countries do not usually get involved. They let the people fight their own battles.

But in 1992, the United Nations sent peacekeepers into Croatia to protect the people and the UN said that no weapons should be sold or given to Yugoslavia. This rule about no selling or giving of weapons to a country is called an *arms embargo*. *Arms* are weapons that can kill and an *embargo* stops or forbids something.

I think Mr. Dr. Jok said that the United Nations also helped make an agreement at the end of 1991 that would help stop the fighting between the Croats and the Serbs in Croatia.

In 1992, BiH, which had a variety of people with different cultures and religions, said that they wanted to be independent from Yugoslavia. Something else that I need to tell you about BiH is that it had a very big population of Muslim people in the country.

Well, Serbia did not want BiH to be independent at all. So the Bosnian Serbs, led by a man named Radovan Karadzic, attacked Sarajevo. Sarajevo is the capital of Bosnia and Herzegovina, and the Serbs and Yugoslav army began killing the Bosnian Muslim people there (they are also called Bosniaks). They began burning Bosniak villages and forcing the Bosniaks to leave their homes so that they could expand Serbia into a bigger area. Other awful things that happened were starving the people, stealing their things after forcing them to leave their homes and doing sick, disgusting things to women and girls.

Since there was an arms embargo, the Bosniaks did not have weapons to fight the Serbs, who had plenty of weapons. So, like in other genocides we have studied, the Serbs got groups of the Bosnian Muslims together and started killing them. These Serbian soldiers made men and boys who were not Serbian go to concentration camps where they were tortured and killed. **All of these horrible things that the Serbs did were called ethnic cleansing.** And what this means was the Serbs were terribly prejudiced against the Bosnian Muslims. So they wanted to get rid of them or clean them away like dirt. **But people are not dirt.** I detest the words ethnic cleansing. They are very disgusting because different groups of people are not dirty and they do not deserve to be wiped away like they are filthy and do not belong.

The world is big enough for everyone to have a place and for everyone to belong.

Okay, so the United Nations gave some help. They sent peacekeepers who gave food and medicine to the Bosnian Muslims. But these peacekeepers were forbidden to do anything to stop the killings—so they kept happening.

In February of 1994, a market area in Sarajevo got attacked. Mortar shells killed almost seventy people and about two hundred others were hurt. Pictures of all of these horrible things got shown on the news all around the world.

Now some action might finally happen!

But even though a group called the North Atlantic Treaty Organization (NATO) demanded that the Serbs get out of Sarajevo and stop their horrible killing plans, more bad stuff kept going on. One of those things—besides more killings—was the capture of some UN peacekeepers. To make sure that no air strikes (this means bombs dropped by planes onto certain places) happened, the Serbs captured hundreds of UN peacekeepers. They chained these peacekeepers to the places where bombs might be dropped. They used people as shields to make sure that they would not be attacked!

The worst killings of people happened in July of 1995 in a region of Bosnia-Herzegovina called Srebrenica (at the time this happened, Bosnia and Herzegovina was called Bosnia-Herzegovina. Bosnia-Herzegovina used to be a province of Yugoslavia when it existed. But the independent state is now called Bosnia and Herzegovina.). Even though the massacre happened in just six days, horrible, sick things were done and a lot of people were left dead.

Under the command of a man named General Ratko Mladic (but that guy Radovan Karadzic was involved in this plan, too), the Serbian forces went into Srebrenica. They got together Bosniak men and boys who were between the ages of about twelve and sixty-five years old. Then they loaded these boys and men into trucks or buses and drove them away to places where they all got shot and killed.

There were about 8,000 of them who were murdered like this.

One of the worst things about Srebrenica was it was supposed to be a "safe haven." Back in 1993, there were six Muslim towns that had been set up by the United Nations to be protected by UN soldiers so the towns would be safe for the people who lived in them. Srebrenica should have been safe from those awful attacks and killings.

But the Bosnian Serbs attacked the safe havens anyway!

Late in 1995, things changed. The Croatian army did an attack against the Serbs, and the Bosnian Muslims got weapons from other Muslim countries so they could fight too. So a lot more killings and fighting happened—and now the Serbs were the ones trying to flee the Croats and the Bosniaks! Also, the United States with other members of that NATO group did a bombing campaign against the Serbs that lasted from the end of August to October of 1995. All of this made the Serb leader, Milosevic, ready to stop this war and talk about peace.

I have to say this right now because it is very important. Mr. Dr. Jok said that that even though the Serbian people had definitely done horrible things during this genocide, the Croat and Bosniak people had also committed atrocities. He explained that this meant that the Croat people and the Bosniaks had also done bad things to the Serb people. He said that there was hate and unfairness and bad things done by all three groups.

By the time the Bosnia-Herzegovina genocide was over, more than 200,000 Bosnian Muslims had been killed. Around two million people had become refugees. A *refugee* is a person who moves from one place to another, usually because something bad is happening in the place where he or she lives.

Oh, here is the end: Some things got settled. A peace plan was made that divided BiH into two parts and set up a government that gave the people a Croat leader, a Serb leader and a Bosniak leader. This is so things would be fair. Some plans got made by the UN Security Council to set up a Yugoslavia tribunal that would deal with those leaders who had thought up and carried out the genocide. Also, nearly 60,000 NATO troops got sent to BiH to make sure that things stayed safe and secure.

The agreement that helped make this peace included the ideas of the Serbs, the Bosniaks and the Croats. The name of this agreement is the *Dayton Accords* because all of the leaders who worked on the plan did so in Dayton, Ohio.

But like Lili always says, the damage had been done. All of those people were dead and the country was all torn up. People were angry and hurt and did not trust each other.

So if you ask me, everybody loses and nobody wins when a genocide happens.

Because the people who kill forget that being a person gives you this amazing chance to be a good person to other people. And the people who get killed are not around anymore to remind us that we should never forget this.

CHAPTER 17

DECEMBER 10, 2008

DEAR J,

It is very early in the morning. The time is 3:09 A.M. But I cannot sleep.

Hombre made me wake up a little while ago. He kept licking my fingers until I sat up in my bed and paid him some attention. His tongue had the feel of the sandpaper that I use to make my wooden sailboats. I make these boats during the summertime. Then I sometimes put blue food coloring in the toilet and let them sail in little circles. But I can only do this when I am sure that Lili or Carmen will not need the bathroom before I can clean up the blue stains.

Anyway, Hombre wanted me to feed him his dog food. I forgot to do this before I went to sleep, so I got up and put food into his bowl. Then to be nice, I gave him three of Carmen's favorite cookies that she thinks she has hidden from me.

Sometimes Carmen is sort of dumb because if there are cookies in my house, I will always find them. It is just something that I am very good at.

But on the way back to my room, I could see that the light in Maker's apartment window was still on. I know it is the window of Maker's family because our family lives across the path from his family. There are not very many apartments in our complex.

It was snowing outside, so I went over to our window and watched the little flakes play chase in the air. Everything was very still. The ground was pure white and glittery and the sky was so black that the bright snowflakes in the air gave me a headache.

I still have my headache.

The light from Maker's window was the color of sunshine on the snow and the yellow glow made it look like his house had a halo all around it. I know about haloes because I sometimes draw pictures of angels with them.

But I do not think that Maker's house has angels or haloes or other stuff like that around it. The light on the snow in the dark just made it look this way.

But here is something strange—and it is probably why I cannot go back to sleep even though Hombre did.

Mrs. Jok came out of that apartment in her robe and slippers. She stood on the porch where me and Maker sometimes play chess and make card houses.

Then she sat down. Even though it was so cold that her breath turned the air into white smoke, she sat on that porch. All by herself.

Then she put her head in her hands and I could see her rocking back and forth the way mothers do when they hold their babies. Except that she was not holding a baby.

After a few minutes, I saw the door open again and even more of that shiny gold light spilled onto the snow. Now Mr. Dr. Jok came out of that apartment. He had on pajamas that were too short and his feet were bare. I thought that he must be very cold.

But he was not paying attention to his pajamas or his feet or the cold smoky air. Instead, he sat down next to Mrs. Jok on that porch. He waited for her to stop rocking. When she did, he wrapped his very long arms around her and pulled her next to him.

That is all. Then Maker's mother and father just sat all scrunched up together on that little snowy porch that glowed in the dark.

And now I am wondering two things:

What could make two people so sad that they would sit alone in the freezing darkness and forget that snow was falling on them like rain?

And what is it about genocide that makes me think that Maker's mother and father have lived through stuff so bad that when they remember what happened, they forget everything else?

✳ ✳ ✳

HELLO JOURNAL—

Now I am back again and it is the same day. Except that it is night now and Maker just left my house. Mr. Dr. Jok came to get him and he did not have on his guard uniform. He had on the same nice clothes that he wore today when he taught Mr. Steinberg's class. But now I know why.

Tomorrow I will tell you about what we are learning in my class. We are studying an African genocide in a country called Rwanda. Rwanda is named the "land of a thousand hills" because it has so many beautiful hills throughout the country.

But I will not talk about Rwanda right now.

I will talk about the conversation that I got to have with Mr. Dr. Jok after school today.

Here is what happened:

After the bell did its ring, I was pushing all of my stuff into my backpack so that I could hurry up and meet Carmen. She was going to walk me home, and if I am late to meet her she will do one of these things: She will roll her eyes when I run up to tell her that I am sorry to be late and then she will yell at me the whole way home. Or the other thing that my mean sister does is she just leaves me to walk home by myself. She does this because she knows I will not tell Papa. I will not tell him because he says that I must be on time and respect the schedules of my sisters. And if I tell, Carmen might get into big trouble, which would be fine by me. But I would also get into some trouble.

So I do not say anything when she leaves me to get home by myself.

Anyway, I was getting my things all situated when Mr. Dr. Jok came over to my desk and just stood there. He did not say anything for a long time. He just watched me pushing my papers and my notebooks into my bag. Then he made a sound like he was trying to get some stuff out of his throat.

I did not know what to do. I felt really stupid just standing there looking at the giant shoes of my best friend's father and listening to him work up gunk from his throat. So I looked up at him. I tried to smile. But that was probably weird because I never give grown ups a smile that makes me look like one of those happy kids with neat hair on the backs of cereal boxes. Those kinds of smiles are a little too sunshiny for me.

But Mr. Dr. Jok did not say anything about my fake smile. He just asked me if I had anything that I wanted to talk about.

I said, no, thank you, very politely and grabbed my backpack so that I could make my getaway. But Mr. Dr. Jok put his hand on my shoulder and asked me to sit down.

I did not want to sit. I wanted to run very fast. I wanted to be an Olympic speed skater like Joey Cheek and just skate away. Except that I did not have on any skates. And my body does not look like Joey Cheek's.

So I sat down in my seat. Mr. Dr. Jok sat down next to me. This was probably very hard for him because he is so tall and his legs are so long, he sort of had to fold himself into a chair.

"You are the best friend of Maker," Mr. Dr. Jok said to me. "You are also a student in this class. And I think that you must be a little confused about why I am teaching it for Mr. Steinberg."

I just shrugged even though I knew that Papa would be annoyed if he knew this. He says shrugging is rude; it is telling people that you do not care about something that might be important to them. I am not allowed to shrug.

But I did it anyway. "No," I said. "I am not confused. I am hungry and I have to meet Carmen."

Mr. Dr. Jok made that disgusting sound in this throat again.

"So you do not wonder what I am doing here? You do not wonder why I came into your classroom the day that you and Maker were standing in the hall while Mr. Thompson spoke angry words to your teacher?"

I knew that Mr. Dr. Jok was smart. He always reads books, and this week I learned he is a doctor who does not wear a long white coat. He is some other kind of doctor because he studied very hard to be an expert in something.

But I did not think that he has a mind like God. Because if God exists, I think he must know everything—like that me and Maker were hiding in that hallway and that I wonder all the time why my best friend's father is now my teacher because Mr. Steinberg has just disappeared. And he disappeared right after that horrible Mr. Thompson told him that it would be good for him to go to a place where genocide is happening—and never, ever come back.

I think about all of these things. They are in my mind, all stuck together the way peanut butter sticks to the top of my mouth when I suck it off of a spoon.

But since I know that Maker's father is just a person and not a god, I am wondering how he knows that I am thinking all of this. I also want to know how he knows that me and Maker were hiding that day he went into the classroom.

I thought that we had been very cool and stealthy like ninjas ready for action.

"Maybe I wonder a little bit," I heard myself say.

Mr. Dr. Jok leaned his body forward in the little chair that he was sitting in. His eyes were very big in his purplish-black face. "Every life is a story, Javier. Every person in this world is born to experience things that will make him both very different from, and very much the same as, the other billions of people on this planet. We are alike and different, and this, my young friend, is a great mystery."

I like mysteries. I check out mystery books at the library all of the time. But I did not really understand how being different and being alike was a mystery.

It just sounded confusing to me.

But since I am known for my politeness, I just nodded my head.

"Javier, I am in this classroom because your teacher is also my professor. Besides teaching the fifth graders at Roosevelt Elementary, Mr. Steinberg also instructs students who attend a university here in Washington. This university trains men and women to work with governments and people all around the world." Mr. Dr. Jok folded his ginormous dark hands together. "Mr. Steinberg is actually Dr. Steinberg, and besides being a very brilliant and kind man, he is also my good friend and professor."

Now I was not just confused. Now I had a million questions. Plus, my head felt all fuzzy and my belly hurt even though I knew that it was not gas.

"Let me explain, Javier. When Achol and I came to America ten years ago, we arrived from Egypt. We were living in Egypt, which is a country in northeast Africa, because we had to get away from a very terrible war that eventually killed more than two million of our people in southern Sudan. So in Egypt, Achol and I both went to university. And when we came to the United States, I knew that I wanted to gain the very best education that I could. I wanted this education so that I could work for peace and understanding in my own country, as well as other lands where I might be compelled to help."

"But I thought that you liked being a security guard in that big building where you work," I said. "Maker said that you liked protecting that building and the people." I knew that I sounded all sulky, but I did not care. All this new information about Maker and his family was freaking me out.

"I did like being a security guard, Javier. To be one who protects people and places, to be a person who helps enforce the laws that govern our cities and states, is a privilege."

"What do you mean, 'you did like' being a guard?" I asked. "Aren't you still a guard? Don't you still wear that cool uniform instead of these fancy clothes that you wear here?" Now I sounded even more sulky and maybe a little snarky. But I did not care.

"I worked as a guard for a long time, my young friend. When Achol and I arrived here, Maker was an infant and my wife and I had experienced...we had lived through great loss and sadness. So I waited a few years before returning to school. In fact, it was your Mr. Steinberg who made the recommendation that I return to university for advanced studies."

I did not know what advanced studies were. I was very confused about Mr. Dr. Steinberg now. And I also did not know why Mr. Dr. Jok was telling me all of this.

I wanted to go. Even though now I would have to walk home by myself because there was no way Carmen would still be waiting for me.

"I think I want to go now," I said as politely as I could. "I am hungry."

Mr. Dr. Jok leaned back in his very small chair and nodded his head. "Then take your leave, Javier."

I did have two more questions, though, and I decided that I would ask them.

"How did you get here? I mean, how did Mr. Steinberg or Mr. Tate choose you to come be our substitute teacher?" I gave Mr. Dr. Jok my best detective look that I sometimes use on Maker when I need for him to know that he had better tell the truth. "And where did my teacher go?"

"Mr. Steinberg is my friend. He was my professor until just a few months ago. Very soon you and your class will know more. But for now, let me say that when his duties made it necessary for him to attend to other things, he asked Mr. Tate if I might instruct your class while he was absent."

"So since you do not guard big buildings anymore, you said 'yes.'" I think that I understood. If Mr. Dr. Jok was not doing his guard work anymore, he must be very bored. And since teaching us fifth graders was not boring, he decided that he would come work with us.

"That is right," Mr. Dr. Jok said. "Since my work has recently become very different, I was free to accept Mr. Tate's offer to teach the fifth graders at Roosevelt Elementary."

"I have one more question."

"You may ask it."

"I have learned that talking about genocide is very tricky. I think that since it is tricky, many people do not like to know very much about it. Because if they know some stuff about it, then they have to decide some things."

Mr. Dr. Jok gave me a look like he was pleased with what I was saying. "What things do you think that they would have to decide?" he asked.

"Well if someone learns that a genocide is happening, then he or she has to decide whether they will be a watcher who just knows about the terribleness or whether they will be a doer, which will mean that even if stuff gets tricky, they will try to help make genocide stop."

"You are right, Javier," Mr. Dr. Jok spoke so quietly that I could hardly hear him. "But what is your question?"

"Well, if it is so tricky, why is it something that Mr. Steinberg and you want to talk about? It seems like genocide is something people might get all mean about—sort of like Mr. Thompson did."

Mr. Dr. Jok thought about my question for a long time and this made me feel very smart.

"Remember I told you that every person has a story?"

I shook my head.

"Well, Javier, I believe—and Mr. Steinberg believes—that because we are all human beings, our stories are meant to be connected and communicated. This means that the things that happen in your life can and should have meaning in the lives of other people you know. And the things that happen in their lives can and should be of importance to you."

I liked the sound of stories all mushing together. But I still did not understand how this would make my teachers want to tell the stories of genocide.

"My story and Mr. Steinberg's story are alike. They are also very different. I will let him tell your class his story when he returns. But some of my story is this: I come from a land where men and women and children were killed in terrible ways. In Sudan, I saw villages on fire and crowds of people running away while very cruel government soldiers shot guns at them. I saw things that were much worse than that, things that still make it very hard for Achol and me to sleep in the night."

I thought about what I had seen at 3:09 A.M. after I gave Hombre his food. I thought about Mrs. Jok's rocking and Mr. Dr. Jok's bare feet on the glowing snowy porch. Maybe they were thinking about those things that make it hard for them to sleep.

"But instead of having hate and being angry at that which is so unjust, I am choosing to work for change. I am choosing to use my experiences, my faith and the education that I have gotten to help people understand that peace and healing can come after war. And many wars and genocides can be prevented if people work together and find ways to handle their disagreements."

My stomach was making fierce noises which meant that I was very hungry. So I stood up and put on my backpack. I thanked Mr. Dr. Jok for telling me all of this stuff.

But just as I got to the door, I had one more question.

"Mr. Jok, what is the hardest thing about genocide? I mean for you, what was the hardest thing?"

Mr. Dr. Jok stared at me for a minute and the way his face looked made my stomach hurt real bad. Then he turned and started walking back to his desk. I could not see his face anymore.

"Maker is our only living son, Javier. But Achol and I had another son and a daughter once."

"Where are they?" I asked.

"They were killed when our village was raided in Sudan. Government soldiers stabbed my daughter with a knife. They shot my son with a gun while I watched and could do nothing."

I just stood there. I know that I must have looked very stupid because I could not think of one word to say to Mr. Dr. Jok. My ears had a ringing sound in them and I could feel my heart pounding.

Then Mr. Dr. Jok turned around. He held his chin high and swallowed very hard. "So remembering how they died and knowing that I will never see them again on this earth is the hardest thing about genocide for me."

CHAPTER 18

DECEMBER 11, 2008

HI J,

I have some news today. And I think that if you were a person you would say "yay." Because what I have to say is way better than just okay...

Remember when I told you that I am creative? Well, now I can prove it!

I AM VERY CREATIVE!!!

The reason that I know this is because I, Javier Ricardo Mendoza, have won the elementary creative writing contest for my whole school district! Out of all the schools that are in my district, I got the award for being the best creative elementary school writer!

Papa does not know yet. He does not know because he has not come home.

Lili does not know either. She is probably in a class or in one of her little groups eating pizza and talking about tests. But she will make a big fuss over me when I tell her. She will probably even give me a big, wet kiss on the cheek that I will wipe off because I have to pretend that her kisses are disgusting. But they are not that bad, really.

I told Carmen because she walked me home after school. I thought that she would say that writing is stupid and that I was just a goofy nerd. But she did not. Instead, she patted my back and told me that I was a smart kid. Then she stopped at this little burrito place that also sells ice cream sandwiches and she bought me one. And she did not even yell at me when I accidentally dropped it on the ground and then picked it back up and ate it anyway.

I think that she was nice to me because I might be famous now. Or sort of famous. Tomorrow, somebody from the big administration building is coming to take my picture and give me some awards. I think that I get to take a creative writing class for free at a Washington, D.C. university this summer (but I do not know which university yet). I also get a first place blue ribbon and maybe a gift card to a book store. But I do not know for sure about the gift card.

If I get a gift card, I will buy books about Africa and dragons. This is because I am worried about some of the wrong things that are happening in some places in Africa (I will tell you more tomorrow because I have lots of notes about Rwanda that I need to write before I lose them). I think that when I get old and finish college, I will try my best to help in these kinds of places. And the reason I want some dragon books is because they interest me.

In fact, I should definitely get dragon books because it was my dragon story that let me be the most creative elementary school writer in my district. But also what let me be the most creative writer is that the judges said I am a master at dialogue.

I did not understand what this meant so Mr. Tate explained it to me. He said that when I wrote my story about dragons and the lands where they lived, I had done a very good job when I made the dragons talk to each other and to the people who tried to capture the lands. *Dialogue* just means the talking that happens between people—and, I guess, dragons.

So I am creative *and* I am a master at dialogue. And I am only in the fifth grade, which means more great things are coming for me.

I might be a writer when I grow up and I will write books about dragons. Then I will sell my books and give money to help groups that are working to make genocide stop.

Yes. This is what I think I will do.

Hey, here is what my story was about: It was about places on those very old maps that have Latin words on them that mean "unknown lands" and "here be dragons." I first saw these words (but I forget the Latin words now) on a picture of some maps in one of Lili's college books. I liked the maps a lot but I did not understand the words. So Lili looked them up with me and we figured out that one map said *unknown lands*, and another map said something like *here be dragons*.

I thought that this was all very weird. But Lili said that the maps were very old. She said that when explorers and mapmakers used to write down where places in the world were, they would only draw what they knew for sure. So if nobody knew about a land or the places in the world that we know about now, they would write *unknown lands* on these unexplored areas.

And some mapmakers (Lili said that a mapmaker is called a *cartographer*) would draw some pictures of dragons on the very edges of their maps. This was probably because they did not know what those uncharted lands were like. And maybe they thought terrible dragons were there to do scary things.

I do not know everything about this. But I decided to write my creative story about unknown lands filled with native people. Then those native people decided to have a journey that went into the lands where there were dragons.

Many things happened in my story and some people and some dragons got killed. But in the end, the unknown lands were not so scary. They were not scary because they were filled with people who had different clothes and hair and powers than we have. But they were still people who had to do some of the same stuff that we do.

And the places where the dragons lived were only scary because they were even further past the unknown lands.

I think people get scared of stuff that they do not understand.

Because the dragons were really very nice and they had good ways of being dragons to each other. And they only breathed their fire or slapped their tails when the natives from the unknown lands came in and tried to do to the dragons what some of the horrible leaders do to the people in lands where genocides happen.

CHAPTER 19

HI J,

It is very cold today. Freezing cold and I cannot make myself warm even though I am wearing two shirts, a sweatshirt and two pairs of socks on my feet. I have decided that cold weather is not fun and that I do not like it except on Christmas.

Here is another thing that I do not like: I do not like machetes.

A machete is a big knife with a very fat blade that will cut plants and weeds into little pieces.

It is also a weapon that can kill and cut up people and animals.

It is the weapon that got used to kill thousands and thousands of people in a country called Rwanda.

I am in my room right now thinking about the genocide in Rwanda. I am also thinking that we have only one more week to study about genocides. Then we have our winter break from school. This will be very fun.

And when I come back to school in January, there will be no more talking about genocide.

But something that bothers me is this: The fifth graders at Roosevelt Elementary might not be talking about genocide anymore. But this does not mean that genocides are not still happening.

While me and my friends and my dog, Hombre, just live our lives and do normal stuff, there will still be people in the world who are living in places where genocide is happening. There will still be people who have to be afraid of riders on horseback and machetes and guns and clubs. There will be people who will be scared to sleep because darkness could bring soldiers who start fires that burn up villages. Night shadows might hide armies that come to kill and steal and drop bombs from airplanes in the sky. And these scared people will not know if they will live or if they will die. They will not know what terrible things they will have to endure if they do not die.

This is all very horrible, and even though I will not be learning or thinking about genocide anymore, it will still be happening. And in the future, there will still be places where it will happen.

When I think about this, it makes me feel all sick and empty inside. Because I get to go on and keep being a normal, creative boy while boys and girls like me die or go through things that are so terrible that they wish that they would not have to live.

Race killing is more than just wrong. It takes away a person's chance to be a person.

What I mean by this is every person who gets born should have a chance to have a whole life. Like Mr. Dr. Jok said, every person has a story. This means that when a baby comes to Earth, it should get to be its whole self. It should get to be an African or an American or an Asian or whatever. It should get to believe what it chooses to believe about stuff like life and faith. It should be free to think for itself and speak its own language and grow up where it is safe and okay to live its life the way it chooses. Even if others are choosing different thoughts and ways.

Every person should have the chance to be a person.

I will have to think some more about the thing that I can do to help make genocides end and stop them in the first place. I will think hard about this because even though I am not very old, I think that I can do something. And if I do this thing and then ask some other plain kids like me to do some things too, maybe something good could happen.

Mr. Steinberg seems to think that everybody's thing that they can do matters. He thinks that even kids can do something.

Speaking of Mr. Steinberg, I wonder where he is. I heard my gym coach, Mr. Tanner, saying something about Mr. Steinberg leaving town suddenly and going somewhere far away. But I think that when he saw me listening with my big ears, he shut his mouth.

I wish that my ears were smaller and did not perk up when I am listening very hard. I know that they perk when I am listening because one time Carmen told me so.

So now I need to talk about Rwanda. I need to write about the genocide that happened there in 1994.

First, here is some stuff about Rwanda.

Rwanda is a little country that is pretty much in the middle of Africa. It is really small and has a lot of hills and is very beautiful. I know that it is beautiful because Mr. Dr. Jok showed us pictures. He told us Rwanda is called the "land of a thousand hills" (I think I already told you this, but I like the sound of it). Also, for its size, Rwanda has more people living in it than any other country in Africa. There are around ten million people in Rwanda and this is a ton of people considering the country is smaller than the state of Massachusetts.

But there were between seven and eight million people living in Rwanda when the genocide started in 1994. The people living there were (and are) mostly from two tribes: the Hutus and the Tutsis. Only a little number (like one percent) of Batwa people live in Rwanda and they have been there for centuries.

Well, there were lots more Hutus in Rwanda than there were Tutsis (Mr. Dr. Jok said that it was like eighty-five percent Hutu and fourteen percent Tutsi). The Hutus were usually peasant farmers while Tutsis were thought of as people who owned cattle. Cattle owners were (and often are) considered more important and powerful, so the Tutsis were thought of as superior to the Hutus. Also, Tutsis were thought to be tall and thin and Hutus were said to be shorter and heavier (but really, it was hard to tell them apart).

This difference between the tribes was not always true, Mr. Dr. Jok told us. Some Hutus had cattle and some Tutsis were farmers—and the Hutus and the Tutsis spoke the same language. Sometimes Hutu and Tutsi people got married and had families together.

Anyway, the thing about Tutsis being better than Hutus was a problem that had gotten much worse during the time when Belgium ruled Rwanda. Up until 1916, Germany had been in charge of Rwanda and Burundi for a while. Burundi is an African country just next to Rwanda and it has mostly Hutu and Tutsi people living there, too.

But during World War I, Belgium conquered these two colonies. A little later, Belgium got formal control of Rwanda and Burundi and ruled them as one country called Ruanda-Urundi until 1962. But since the Tutsis were said to be natural leaders, they got to be the local rulers over the Hutus.

So, the Belgian rulers egged on this idea that Tutsis were better and more civilized than Hutus. Then in the early 1930s, the rulers started making both tribes carry identification cards. These identification cards were small cards that told the name of the person carrying it. The cards also said whether the person was a Hutu or a Tutsi.

All of these things caused stress between the tribes. So a lot of fighting happened between the Hutus and Tutsis way before the genocide in 1994. There were also many changes to the people in charge in both Rwanda and Burundi.

In 1959, there was a big Hutu revolution and Rwanda's local leaders got switched. Instead of Tutsis being in charge, now the Hutus were the bosses. After this, there were a bunch more big fights between the two tribes and thousands of people kept getting killed.

On July 1, 1962, Rwanda and Burundi both got to be free from Belgium. Now they were independent and could rule themselves.

Well, with the Hutus being in charge, the Tutsi people got treated badly. And since so many Tutsis had already run away to Uganda (which is a country right next to Rwanda) because the Hutus were fighting against them, the Tutsis made up their own army called the Rwandan Patriotic Front (RPF). The leaders of the RPF trained mostly Tutsi soldiers while they were living in the refugee camps in Uganda.

There are many refugee camps in some countries in Africa (but definitely not in all African countries). These camps are not like summer camp where you go to have fun. They are not camps where you roast marshmallows and sleep in big green tents. *Refugee camps* are places where people go when there are big dangerous fights between groups in their countries. And like I said earlier, a *refugee* is a person who hurries from their own country where there is war or danger to another country that they hope will be safer. In refugee camps, the refugees live very close together and get a lot of their food and water and clothes from humanitarian aid groups. These camps are not very nice and the people who live in them often get diseases and have fights of their own.

Anyway, the Tutsi-led RPF went out of Uganda and invaded Rwanda in 1990. But France and other countries were helpful to the Rwandan government and the RPF did not get to take charge of Rwanda.

Now the Rwandan government leaders and Hutu President Juvenal Habyarimana were really mad. They started encouraging brutal behavior against the Tutsis. Something else that the government did was start training groups of young men to fight against the Tutsis. This group of soldiers that would later kill was called the *Interahamwe*. Interahamwe means those who work or fight together. Besides supporting the Interahamwe, the Rwandan government started using the radio and newspaper to spread anti-Tutsi propaganda. There were pogroms, too, which was a lot like what happened to the Jews by the Nazis.

The fights between the Hutus and the Tutsis got worse, so some Western governments tried to help make some peace. Finally in August of 1993, in the town of Arusha (which is in Tanzania), President Habyarimana went to some talks about peace for his country. After some talking, he accepted an agreement that said he would share his power with the RPF. This agreement was called the *Arusha Accords.*

When we talked about this agreement in my class, I thought that maybe all the killings in the past between the Hutus and the Tutsis were the genocide in Rwanda. I mean, thousands and thousands of people had been killed. So I thought that maybe the peace treaty that got signed by the Rwandan government and the RPF would mean everyone would get along better.

I was wrong.

A lot of people in the Rwandan government did not want to share their power with the Tutsis. So to keep more fighting from happening, and to make sure that stuff in the Arusha Accords actually got practiced, the United Nations Security Council sent peacekeepers to Rwanda. A man from Canada named Romeo Dallaire was in charge of these soldiers. At first, there was less, but at the biggest, there were 2,500 UN peacekeepers in Rwanda.

Meanwhile, the Rwandan government had been busy buying and storing up things like tons of machetes and guns and axes and grenades. They had been doing this for a while. Also, the young men in the Interahamwe were being trained to kill people very fast. At the same time, lists of Tutsis and where they lived were being made. In the schools, children got split into two separate groups—Hutus and Tutsis. And the people of Rwanda still carried those identification cards that said whether they were Hutus or Tutsis.

General Dallaire found out about the collection of machetes and stuff. He also learned about some Hutu government plans to kill ten Belgian peacekeepers. So he called some UN leaders in New York. New York is where the UN has its headquarters. Dallaire told them that he wanted to go in and get all of the stored weapons to keep big horrible killings from happening.

But his UN bosses said no—and they forbid him to go and get the weapons. And every time Dallaire tried to do something that would stop the coming genocide, the UN told him he could not do the thing that was needed to protect the people. The UN also would not send more troops to Rwanda even though Dallaire asked for them.

The genocide started on April 6, 1994. It started when the plane that was carrying President Habyarimana and Burundi's president, Cyprien Ntaryamira, got shot down by missiles.

Both of these presidents were killed and no one knows for sure who fired the missiles.

Anyway, right after the crash, the Hutu government troops, Interahamwe soldiers and presidential guard started killing Hutu leaders who would not be willing to murder Tutsis. Then they started carrying out their big plan of killing all of the Tutsi people that they could.

On April 7th, the prime minister and her husband were killed. Ten of the Belgian peacekeepers who were in charge of watching over them got murdered, too. This caused the other Belgian troops to be removed from Rwanda. Other countries also took away the peacekeepers that they had sent, and pretty soon Dallaire's team was very small and it could not do much to stop the genocide.

Now the killings were really happening. They were happening very fast.

It was all very crazy if you ask me—and very, very sick. Many Hutu people did not dislike or hate Tutsi people. But these

Hutus who did not want to hurt the Tutsis got forced to kill anyway. The Hutu government soldiers and the Interahamwe made these Hutus kill their Tutsi friends and their neighbors and even people who were part of their families. If these Hutus refused to kill Tutsis, then they would be murdered!

So the killings were wild and all kinds of people became the executioners. The killers murdered with guns and axes and those machetes—and they hacked people to death. These Hutus killed like they were out of their minds and they murdered everywhere they went—even in places like churches and schools and other areas where lots of Tutsis would gather to try and be safe. At these places, they would do horrible killings of hundreds and hundreds of people at a time. The things that they did to the women and the girls were so detestable I cannot even write about it. But many Hutu soldiers would get together and do the most awful things to women and girls.

These terrible crimes against girls and women had happened during other genocides. And the awfulness of them is so bad that it makes me want to throw up even though I hate to vomit up stuff from my belly.

I need to tell you about some Hutus so that you do not think that they all became killers.

Like I said, some Hutus did not hate Tutsis. They did not want to see Tutsi people killed. In fact, some Hutus protected Tutsi people by hiding them and trying to trick Hutu government soldiers and Interahamwe militia.

A man who did this was Paul Rusesabagina. Mr. Rusesabagina was Hutu, his wife was Tutsi, and he was a manager at a very important and fancy hotel in Kigali, Rwanda. To make a long story sort of short, Paul R. used his job and all of his relationships that he had with Hutu military leaders to protect more than 1,200 Tutsis and some Hutus who did not want to kill Tutsis.

What he did was not easy because the Hutu killers started wanting to get into the hotel to get at the people who had come to be safe. But Mr. Rusesabagina used all of his abilities to protect the people even when no help came from the United Nations or the outside world. His story got turned into a movie called *Hotel Rwanda*, but Papa says that I cannot see this movie yet. Lili agrees with him and so it is final. I will have to see it when I get even more grown up.

But I think that Paul Rusesabagina is brave. His life makes me think about how I would act if killers were trying to murder people around me. Would I help them and try to keep them safe? Would I let myself be killed because I was trying to protect other people?

I really do not know what I would do. I would like to think that because I have cool ninja plans and shoes that do not squeak when I run that I would use my powers to do good and right.

I would like to think that because I know that race killing is more horrible than I can say that I would protect people the way that Mr. Rusesabagina did or the way Oskar Schindler did when he helped save the lives of more than 1,200 Jewish people during the Holocaust.

I would like to think that I would be like William Wilberforce (we have learned about these doers from Mr. Dr. Jok), who spent a ton of his life working to outlaw the British slave trade that would eventually end slavery in the British Empire. I would like to be like Harriett Tubman, who guided a raid when she was in the Union Army that freed hundreds of slaves. I think it would be cool to be like Martin Luther King, who stuck up for all people to have the same rights and treatment as others.

Every person should have the right to be a person without having to worry about being destroyed or treated badly.

Now back to Rwanda. These brutal killings happened for 100 days throughout the country. The United Nations did not send help even though General Dallaire kept asking and asking for it. In fact, all but 500 UN peacekeepers left Rwanda (only 270 were supposed to stay behind, but some soldiers would not leave). Other humanitarian groups like the Red Cross kept telling about the killings in Rwanda. So since news of the genocide was a fact, and the horrible story of it was on the news all around the world, that UN Security Council said it was going to send 5,500 soldiers to Rwanda.

But the help never came on time.

Eventually the RPF army beat the Hutu army and the Interahamwe soldiers. But by then, at least 800,000 people had been killed and probably around two million Hutu killers ran away across borders into Burundi, Uganda, Tanzania and the Democratic Republic of the Congo (DRC). This helped cause more fighting—and war in DRC (which was called Zaire then).

Fighting still keeps happening there even though the last big war was supposed to have ended a long time ago.

The man who led the RPF is now the president of Rwanda. His name is Paul Kagame. So things are a lot better in Rwanda, but so much was destroyed there. So many people were killed. Just like other genocides, a lot of men got killed first, so there are not as many men as women in Rwanda. This creates a lot of problems. And it seems to me that trying to put this country back together again must be sort of like trying to get Humpty Dumpty all fixed up after he had his big fall.

I guess healing from genocide takes a long time.

But that United Nations Security Council did create what is called the International Criminal Tribunal for Rwanda (ICTR) to help bring peace to the country and make the people responsible for the genocide have to answer for their terrible crimes. The Tribunal is in Arusha, Tanzania and some big decisions have been made to punish some of the major planners and doers of this genocide.

Probably the very biggest planner and boss in this genocide is a Hutu leader named Theoneste Bagosora. After President Habyarimana was killed, Theo (I'm calling him this for short) had the prime minister, her husband and the ten Belgian peacekeepers murdered. Then he was pretty much in charge of the Hutu military and the Interahamwe—and he gave tons of orders to kill. The ICTR said he was guilty of a lot of crimes, including genocide. He has to spend the rest of his life in prison.

Also, a very good and special decision got made by this court that has to do with the crimes done to the bodies of women and girls. A man named Jean-Paul Akayesu, who had ordered killings and terrible things done to girls and women, got convicted and sentenced to spend the rest of his life in prison. And a decision was made that said those things that were done to the bodies of women and girls were now considered to be one of the things that make up genocide! Also, more decisions are supposed to be coming about some others who were involved in all of this. If the ICTR says that these people are guilty, they will be punished.

So there have definitely been some trials and punishments that have happened. Things are just taking a very long time.

Another thing that is happening to help heal Rwanda is something that the people call gacaca courts. *Gacaca* is an old and traditional form of setting things right in local communities. These courts are a way of having people who have committed crimes have to face the people who they have hurt. If the people who were hurt are now dead, the criminal has to face the families of those people—often in the places where they committed the crimes.

Since there were more than 100,000 people in prisons for taking part in Rwanda's genocide, the gacaca courts got set up by the Rwandan government. They were set up to help decisions get made about some of these prisoners. Because just normal people in the community listen to the trials of those who committed crimes during the genocide, it gives the victims a chance to have others hear the truth. These people get to see the criminals have to answer for what has been done.

Judges of the gacaca courts are picked by the local people. These judges get chosen because they are known to be honest and fair. But they also get some training. They get this training to help them make the best choices that they possibly can about things.

Some other things happen in gacaca courts that are supposed to bring healing and more peace to the people. The person who has done wrong things can confess what he or she has done and then have to face the punishment for it. But also, the person who did wrong might tell the people who he or she has hurt that he is sorry and that he wants to be forgiven.

I do not know too much more about gacaca courts except to say that there are thousands of them in Rwanda. And people have different ideas about how they will help make things right after this awful genocide.

I hope that they will help.

Mr. Dr. Jok said that it is important for things to be made as right and fair as possible when genocides happen (even though he also said that there is nothing that could ever make the horrible stuff that happened okay). And he said that a very big part of things being set straight has to do with forgiveness. He said that forgiveness does not mean that the person who did horrible things gets to go free from his crime. It does not mean that the victim of a criminal has to forget the terrible stuff that has happened to him and his family. And it definitely does not mean that the awful things that happened are okay.

Forgiveness just means that the person who got hurt decides that he or she will not hold hate and anger and a plan to get even in their heart.

I think forgiving sort of means that even though you were all broken or crushed by something really bad that you use what is left of your energies to try and get whole again. Even if you only get whole in a broken kind of way.

And forgiveness helps the hurt person get more free. Because if you get all busy hating the people who hurt you and making plans to get even, the madness takes up your energy and makes your mind full of dark plans.

But by forgiving, the hurt person gets free to go on with his life and let what is right and fair get worked out in the courts or wherever. Because, like I said, forgiving someone does not mean that the person who did wrong will not have a consequence for the bad things that they have done.

Papa always says that people reap what they sow. I asked him what this means and he told me that it just means that you will harvest what you plant.

If a farmer plants apple seeds, he will get an apple tree and some apples after a while. If I plant some marigold seeds in the little garden box on my porch, I will get bright orange and red marigolds (if snails do not eat them up first).

But I will not get apples if I plant marigolds. And the farmer would not get marigolds if he plants apple seeds.

This is also true of the things that we do, Papa says. If we do good and choose right, our lives will have peace and a clear conscience. Other good things might happen, too.

But if we choose wrong and cruel and greedy ways of living, these choices eventually catch up with us, too.

So if we want to harvest things like peace and kindness and safety, we should try to forgive and be fair. We should try to work for justice in places where maybe things are not so fair.

And maybe the people who get whole again in that broken kind of way are some of the best people to help other people move on with their lives after something as horrible as genocide.

CHAPTER 20

DECEMBER 15, 2008

HELLO J,

I just want to tell you that I know something is very true about me. I have always thought that this thing might be so, but I was not for sure.

Now I know it.

I am a strange boy.

I am not strange because I am creative and polite and maybe even noble. I am not strange because of my large soft belly and my big ears.

I am strange because when something gets into my brain, I cannot get it out. The something sticks around in my head just like a piece of taco meat does when it gets all stuck in between my teeth and I cannot get it out even with my tongue.

All this weekend, I could not get Rwanda out of my head. I could not make genocide go away from my mind.

So I have made up a plan that I will tell to Mr. Dr. Jok tomorrow. And I will ask him to ask Mr. Tate about my plan if he thinks it is a good one.

My plan has to do with being a doer who gets involved instead of just watching the terrible things that happen with genocide.

So I am strange for sure because boys like me do not usually sit around and think about stuff that they learn in class and then get all busy making plans about things like genocide.

But I am okay with my strangeness, and when I told Lili about my plan and about how I am weird, she said that I was wrong. She said that I am not strange. She said that I am choosing to care about things that matter. She said that she was very proud of me and that Mr. Dr. Steinberg would be proud, too.

I do not know about this. But I will tell you more tomorrow after I talk with Mr. Dr. Jok.

This is our last week of learning about genocides. Today is Monday and we talked about the genocide in Sudan.

Sudan is the biggest country in Africa. It is the tenth largest country in the world!

Sudan has a population of about forty million people, and the Nile River, which is the longest river in the world, runs through it. I think Mr. Dr. Jok said the Nile was like 4,186 miles long.

The country is divided mostly into north and south (but we will talk about the west, too). The north is very dry and desert-like because the Sahara Desert goes through it. The capital of Sudan, which is Khartoum, is in the north.

The south is more tropical-like and it has woodlands and swamps and lots of wildlife in some places.

But these are not the only differences between the north and south parts of Sudan.

The north is where the main government of Sudan has been for a long time. The president of Sudan is a man named Omar al-Bashir, and he is a person who has caused horrible things to be done to the people in the south of Sudan. He has also caused sick and awful things to be done against the people in the west of Sudan—in Darfur. Maybe in the east, too, but we are not learning about this area of the country.

The people in the north part of Sudan are Arabs, which means that their ancestors came from an area that has been known as Arabia. Many Arab people (but not all) are followers of the religion Islam and they speak the Arabic language. This is definitely true about Omar al-Bashir and his government of Sudan, which is now called the National Congress Party.

But the people in the south of Sudan are black Africans. They are either animists, which means that their religion comes from their tribal practices, or they are Christians. There are hundreds of different tribes in southern Sudan and hundreds of languages that are spoken in these tribes. But the two major tribes in southern Sudan are the Dinka and the Nuer tribes.

Anyway, there has been terrible fighting between Sudan's north and south since the country got to be free from British and Egyptian colonial rulers in 1956 (there was fighting even before this time, too). Some of the reasons for fighting have been about differences in religion (the north wants the south to follow the teachings of Islam) and prejudice about race (the Arab government in northern Sudan thinks that they are superior to the black people in the south). And like I wrote about a long time back, there have been huge killings of the black Africans in the south because there are so many natural resources in the south that the north wants.

So there has been awful fighting in the south since before 1956, with only about thirteen or fourteen years of peace. The first peaceful period came from between 1972 and 1983. It was when an agreement got put in place that let the people in the south be in charge of themselves. The agreement was called the *Addis Ababa Agreement* (Addis Ababa is the capital of Ethiopia, which is next to Sudan) because this is the place where the agreement got worked out.

But then the government in the north changed their minds. In September of 1983, they started trying to force the south to follow Islamic law (called sharia law), which the southerners did not believe in. The northern Sudanese government began to go into the south and burn up the villages and kill the men and take the women back to the north part of Sudan. They would take these southern Sudanese women and girls and do those horrible things to them. They would also make them into slaves.

Well, the people in the south did not just sit around and let these awful things happen. A southern Sudanese man named Dr. John Garang got together a group of men and older boys. These men and boys trained and became soldiers. Together they fought the attacks of the north and they called themselves the Sudan People's Liberation Army (SPLA). They fought to be free from the cruel ways of Sudan's northern government, which was then called the National Islamic Front. They fought to protect themselves and their families and the land that they lived on.

But Mr. Dr. Jok said that we had to remember that the SPLA was not an army of angels. The men and older boys sometimes did very bad things. He said that whenever there is fighting between groups, wrong things happen on all sides. This is true even if a group is trying to protect itself from being taken over by brutal soldiers and government leaders like Omar al-Bashir.

Between the years 1983 and 2005, more than 2.5 million southern Sudanese people got killed and more than five million of them lost their homes and had to go to other places. Some of these places were (and still are) the countries of Kenya, Ethiopia, Egypt, Uganda and other areas in Sudan. Many of the people who became refugees had to live in refugee camps.

But the SPLA's hard work was not for nothing. In 2005, a peace agreement called the *Comprehensive Peace Agreement* got signed between al-Bashir's northern government, which is now called the National Congress Party, and the southern SPLA. Together the new shared government between the north and south is called the *Government of National Unity*. And the agreement that got signed says that the north has to share its power with the south. It also says that the oil that the north had been taking away from the south has to be shared. The money that the northern government was getting by selling the oil that was in the south has to be divided with the people in the south.

Also, the north cannot force its religion on the people in the south anymore. The southern Sudanese people can believe what they choose to believe about faith and God.

There are some other things in this agreement that are supposed to happen. But Mr. Dr. Jok said that a number of these things are not happening like they should be. Omar al-Bashir and his leaders are interrupting the fairness that should be making things better for the people in the south.

Also, after more than twenty years of war, southern Sudan is pretty much destroyed. When our class looked at the pictures that Mr. Dr. Jok showed us, we could see that there are almost no roads with pavement on them in the southern cities (there are not even very many dirt roads). The people mostly live in mud huts. Many cannot get clean water to drink, and there are hardly any doctors or places to go when a person gets sick. Also, there are not very many schools because during the war, the schools and hospitals and villages all got ruined by bombs and guns and fire. A lot of people are very hungry and some of them do not even wear clothes.

There are a lot of humanitarian groups in southern Sudan that are trying to help the people. And since this peace agreement, the people of the south have been busy trying to rebuild their land and communities. So progress is definitely happening, Mr. Dr. Jok says.

But it will take a lot of time. It will also mean that the peace agreement works and that no more fighting starts. **Because if war starts again, any new buildings and fixing up of stuff that has happened in southern Sudan will get destroyed again.**

I feel very sad about this genocide because a lot of people and governments around the world did not pay attention to all of the killings and terrible destruction that happened in southern Sudan. Many people and countries did not even call it genocide.

I guess it was sort of the same with Armenia and with the Holocaust. It was also what happened in Cambodia and Bosnia and Rwanda.

The world does not seem to care very much until it is too late.

Even though we have rules about genocide and about how race killing should be prevented and punished. **But Mr. Dr. Jok told us that there are many people who do care.** There are people who spend their lives working to tell the stories of people and countries that are being treated unjustly. These men and women (and even some teenagers) work with people in their own governments to try and make laws that bring fairness and protection to places that are being hurt by unfair governments. They also work to get other people (mostly just plain ordinary people) involved so that they will become doers who stick up for the people being hurt or killed.

. Because of the work of these kinds of people, good things do happen. These people help their governments get involved. They put pressure on certain organizations and groups and world leaders who can help influence the choices of unjust leaders. They also put pressure on the leaders of the United Nations and try to get the UN involved.

But Mr. Dr. Jok said that the UN needs to do a better job of interrupting and ending genocide. That Security Council should remember the Genocide Convention and then do what needs to happen when governments start hurting their own people.

Something else that Mr. Dr. Jok said should happen is there needs to be laws that all countries in the world have to follow when it comes to natural resources. Having ways that everybody has to obey when it comes to getting things like oil and gold and minerals and timber would help stop sneaky government leaders from hurting their own people.

Now I am tired of writing about genocide.

But before I stop, I will tell you about Darfur. The reason I will do this is because I want to be done telling about all of these genocides. So if I write down the awful stuff that is happening in Darfur, then I will be mostly done. Maybe I will have time to just write down some other things that happen in class and about my plan that I have.

So about Darfur:

Darfur is in the west part of Sudan. It is a big area that is about the size of France and it is divided into three states: West Darfur, South Darfur and North Darfur. The word *Darfur* means "land or area of the Fur." But the Fur is not like the hair on an animal. Fur is the name of one of the largest tribes in the area of Darfur. The other main tribes are called the Masalit and the Zaghawa tribes. In these tribes are black African people who are mostly followers of Islam.

Anyway, Darfur was all by itself for hundreds of years and it was ruled by sultans. Sultans were (and sometimes still are) like the kings of Muslim countries. But eventually, Darfur got included as part of Sudan during the time when the Egyptian and British governments ruled Sudan.

Darfur is very dry and sandy, especially in the north because of the Sahara Desert being there. But in southern Darfur, everything can get greener during the rainy season.

Well, before Sudan got to be free from its British and Egyptian colonial bosses, these rulers mostly just paid attention to the north area of Sudan, which was populated with Arab people. The black people in the south and the west did not get much attention. The rulers did not spend a lot of time or money helping develop their lands.

So the people in Darfur got left out. The north part of Sudan got all of the attention, and later on, the people from the north got to have all of the power.

This made the people who lived in Darfur feel angry and disappointed.

And when the Darfurians (which means the people of Darfur) saw that the big war between Sudan's north and south might end, and there could finally be some good things happening to the black southern Sudanese, they were very angry. They were angry because they felt like they had been mistreated and forgotten by Sudan's Arab northern government, too. They felt like they deserved to have some power and some chances to make changes that would help the area of Darfur.

So in early 2003, a group of angry men from Darfur attacked a military set-up that belonged to the northern Sudanese government. The military set-up, called an outpost, was in Darfur.

Well, the northern Sudanese government (which was still known as the National Islamic Front then) did something horrible. I will tell you about the terribleness of what they did. But first I have to explain about the different people in Darfur.

The black people in Darfur were usually farmers. They farmed whatever good land they could get in Darfur.

There were also some Arab people who lived close to this area, and they usually had some animals that they moved around with so the animals could graze for food. These Arab *nomads* (nomads are people who go from place to place) were herdsmen because they herded their animals to and from different areas.

Anyway, this all was pretty much okay. Besides some little fights about animals and crops and sort of getting in each other's way, these Arab people and black people had mostly gotten along.

But when the angry Darfuri men attacked an NIF military base, the northern Sudanese government started getting the Arab herdsmen to do terrible work for them. This awful work that the NIF wanted them to do was to go into hundreds of black villages in Darfur and burn them up. They wanted the black people of Darfur to be killed so they gave the Arab herdsmen some camels and horses and big guns. They trained them how to use these weapons. Then they commanded them to murder the people of Darfur.

These herdsmen who did (and still do) this are called the Janjaweed. *Janjaweed* means "devils on horseback." The Janjaweed gets its support and things from the NIF, which is now called the National Congress Party (NCP). I already said this, but the NCP is the Arab-Islamic northern government of Omar al-Bashir that used to be called the National Islamic Front (NIF).

The things that have happened to the black people in Darfur are so terrible that I cannot make my mind understand it. The

Janjaweed and the northern government soldiers have worked together to destroy hundreds of villages. They do this by burning the little huts of the people and killing the men by shooting them with guns. Sometimes they use other weapons. They even kill little tiny babies in the most horrible ways while their parents watch and cannot do anything about it.

Then many soldiers from both the Janjaweed and from the northern Sudanese government do sick, evil things to the women and the girls.

Another awful thing that the NCP has done is bomb the villages using helicopters and other kinds of planes. While the people in the Darfurian villages try to run away as their homes and communities are being burned up, the NCP drops bombs from the sky to cause more deaths and destructions.

The NCP did the same thing in southern Sudan (but they were called the NIF back then).

I could tell you much more stuff about Darfur. We got to read some books that had some things about southern Sudan and Darfur in it. The stories made me very angry and sad. They made me want to be a real superhero who could just go in and grab up all the killers in Darfur and put them in a prison so they could not hurt anymore people.

Genocide makes me angry.

The numbers of dead people in Darfur are hard to know, Mr. Dr. Jok told us. But he said that up to a half million people (mostly from those three major tribes) have been killed or have died in the past almost-six years. And more than 2.5 million Darfuri people have lost their homes because nearly all of their villages have been destroyed (like eighty to ninety percent of them, I think).

A lot of the Darfurian people have run across the Sudan border into the countries of Chad and sometimes the Central African Republic. They live in refugee camps there and get help from the UN and other humanitarian aid groups. Some Darfuris live in other parts of Darfur in what are called internally displaced people camps, or IDP camps. *Internally displaced people* is a big expression that means the people inside of a country who have been forced by war or conflict to leave their homes and move to another part of their country. Refugees move from their country to another country. But an internally displaced person stays inside their country. This person just moves to another part of it that is safer.

· But the Darfuri people are not even safe in these camps. The camps often do not have much food or water and many people get bad diseases. A lot of times, those Janjaweed soldiers will actually come to the camps and destroy those, too!

Not that much has been done to help the people in Darfur. Even though the United States called all of these killings "genocide" in September of 2004, and countries all around the world have reported massive destruction and deaths, nothing big has been done by the UN to make it all stop.

That UN Security Council did vote to send in some peacekeepers to help a group of African soldiers that are trying to keep peace in Darfur. The group of soldiers is called the African Union, and the men in it are from different African countries. They come to help when there is war or fighting in another African country.

But the African Union troops were too small and they did not have what they needed to protect the people of Darfur. They were not able to help bring about peace and safety.

So in July of 2007, after some other things that were tried to help bring peace, the UN Security Council voted to send a peacekeeping force that was to be made up of both UN peacekeepers and African Union peacekeepers. The team altogether would be called UNAMID. UNAMID stands for "United Nations African Mission in Darfur" and it would have 26,000 peacekeepers in it.

But so far, only 11,500 have gone to help (even though there are supposed to be about 15,000 peacekeepers by the end of this month).

And even though there have been some more actions to try and get peace in Darfur, it is a very big mess there. Some of this mess is because the Darfuri groups that wanted to be treated equally in the first place have broken into lots of other little groups. These little groups are fighting each other about what they want while Omar al-Bashir and his northern government keep ordering horrible things to be done to the people of Darfur. Al-Bashir says that he is not involved in these terrible killings just like he said that he and his government were not responsible for what happened in southern Sudan.

He is not telling the truth.

So with all of the fighting between the people of Darfur and the horrible deeds of the Janjaweed, plus the denying that is being done by al-Bashir's NCP, peace is not happening. The killings have not stopped even though there are not as many as in the beginning of all of this.

Still, a genocide is happening again and this seems totally crazy to me. It seems crazy because I think that the Genocide Convention that got signed by those UN members in 1948 (and now there are 140 countries that have ratified it) says that when genocide is happening, the world has to stop watching and do something about it. Genocide is a crime and it is against international law.

And even though this is true, nothing is happening to stop it in Darfur.

That is all I have to say about this for now. I am very tired from all of this writing and I am upset. I am upset because at the end of this week I will be done learning about genocide while the people in Darfur have to go on living in a place where even those fierce dragons on old maps would be terrified to go.

CHAPTER 21

DEAR BOOK ABOUT GENOCIDE,

Mr. Dr. Jok liked my plan and he told it to Mr. Tate, who now thinks that I am smarter than ever!

In fact, they both like my plan so much, they are going to tell it to all of the families of Roosevelt Elementary. Liliana and Papa are SO proud of me, and even Carmen is being nice to me. I think that she is being nice because if I get all famous, she will want me to give her my autograph that says something about me really being her brother.

Anyway, this is my cool plan. It is my plan to do what I can to help stop genocide and keep new ones from starting.

I am going to get some t-shirts made. Then I will sell them. Then I will give the money from my t-shirts to some groups in Washington, D.C. that are doing this work, too.

My t-shirts will not be normal t-shirts. I mean they will be nice and all, but they will also have some special words on them about genocide.

Here is how my idea happened:

I was talking to Lili on Saturday about genocide. I was telling her about what I had learned. I told her about a lot of the things in my journal and I told her that we would finish our studies about race killing in one week. But the people who are living with genocide will not be so lucky.

Then I told her about Mr. Steinberg saying that everybody could do something. I told her how he said that we all could find a thing that we could do to help—and then do it.

My big sister is the coolest big sister in the world (I am not talking about Carmen, just Lili). She told me that I was a kind, smart boy and that my teacher is right: Everybody *can* do something. So she asked me what I thought I could do. She asked me to tell her the thing that I thought I might do to help. I told her that I did not know. But I said that I did not want to just be a watcher. I want to be a doer that sticks up for people who cannot defend themselves from genocide bullies like those we have been learning about.

So Lili asked me to name some good things that I could do. I told her about writing to people in Congress and about writing to our president. I said that it would be good to get groups of people together and teach people about genocide. And I said that maybe I could make some money and then send it to groups that help fight genocide and groups that give aid to people in places where war and genocide are happening.

Then my smart sister asked me how I could make this money. I would have to do something creative if I was going to make some money to send.

This made me think about t-shirts. I like t-shirts a lot. I wear them almost every day because I have agreed to Papa's rules about t-shirts: I must tuck them in neatly and all of my t-shirts have to say good things on them.

All of a sudden, I knew the thing that I could do! I told Lili that I could make some t-shirts that say something about genocide on them. I could go to the store and spend all the money I have saved (which is $62.47) and buy t-shirts and permanent markers. Then I could write good stuff on them and sell them to Maker and some of my other friends. I could make them cost $6.45 or something.

Liliana said that my idea was a very good one. But she also had an idea that might help. Her idea was to call one of her university friends from those little study groups. The friend that she said she would call is Bao Huynh and he owns a little t-shirt company that designs t-shirts for lots of different groups. Maybe Bao could help me with my plan, she said

So I said that she could call Bao and she did. On Sunday, Bao came to my house and we sat at my kitchen table. Me and Lili and him all sat together and they talked to me like I was a grown up. They asked me my ideas and they listened to me go on and on about how genocide is so terrible and horrible and that it needs to stop.

Then Bao said that he was going to do something that he usually does not do. He said he was going to make the t-shirts that I could design with him, and he was going to give me fifty free shirts that I could sell to whoever I wanted. He said that maybe I could even talk to my teacher. I could see if my school wanted to help sell them since studying genocide was their idea in the first place.

I told Bao that if he gave me free shirts that his little company might get poor because fifty shirts is a lot of shirts to give for free. But he said that I did not need to worry about this. He said that sometimes it is important to make some sacrifices when those sacrifices can help other people.

He told me and Lili that this was the thing that he could do to help end genocide.

So I told him thank you and then we worked on my shirts. This is what they look like: The t-shirt is sort of a dark tan. It looks like wet sand. And the letters that Bao is going to put on the shirt are chocolate brown and rust-red. I know the names *chocolate brown* and *rust-red* because Bao showed me some colors on a card that I could choose from, and the ones that I picked had these names.

There are words on the front and words on the back of my t-shirts. This is what my shirt looks like:

The front of my t-shirt

Do the thing that YOU can do

The back of my t-shirt

I am very happy about this t-shirt because it says all of the names of the countries we studied (even though I know that a lot more places in the world have had genocides) and then on the front it says the best thing ever: ***Do the thing that YOU can do...***

I think that Mr. Steinberg would be proud if he is not dead. I am worried that he is not alive anymore because there is still Mr. Dr. Jok for my teacher.

But anyway, I told this idea to Mr. Dr. Jok yesterday and I showed him the picture of the shirts that Bao is making for me to sell. And he liked my idea so much that he told Mr. Tate right away. Then today, Miss Bell came to my class to get me, and since she is Mr. Tate's secretary, I got sent with her to the school office immediately.

At first I felt all scared because nobody told me why I had to go. I thought maybe my principal found out about the day that me and Maker listened to Mr. Thompson scream at Mr. Steinberg. I thought that maybe Mr. Tate now thought that me and Maker were school moles and that we were dangerous.

But Mr. Tate came right out of his office to meet me. He had a big smile on his face so I knew that I was probably not wanted for being a mole.

Well, to make a long story sort of short, Mr. Tate was all happy about my t-shirt idea. In fact, he told me that he has very good plans for this great idea of mine.

Then because I am such a polite and noble boy, I told my principal that I was not the only person who had worked on my t-shirt idea. My sister, Lili, and her friend, Bao, had each done a thing that they could do, too. Lili had listened to me and cared about what I said. Then she had called Bao.

Bao had listened to me and cared about genocide, too. He had cared enough to give me fifty nice shirts for free that I can sell so that I will have money to give away.

My principal said that what I was doing was the very thing that he and Mr. Dr. Steinberg had hoped that the students at Roosevelt Elementary would do. He said that because I understood and cared about how serious and terrible genocide is, I was choosing to be a doer. I was choosing to do the thing that I could do to help.

So Mr. Tate said that he was going to talk to some of his bosses and see if Roosevelt Elementary could sell the t-shirts for the whole school and maybe even some other schools in Washington, D.C.

I thought this was very good news. The reason that I thought this was good news was because maybe the shirts can tell more people about genocide. And then the money from the shirts can go to smart groups that are doing work to stop and prevent genocides. Papa also said that I can learn about some universities and seminaries that have special reconciliation programs. I can maybe send some money to them, too. *Reconcile* means to make a relationship good and new again, especially if the relationship got all broken by things that were wrong and unfair. And some universities and seminaries (seminaries are places where people go to study about the ways of God) have some good reconciliation studies that train people to help bring understanding and healing between people in places like Bosnia and Sudan.

Oh, and some extra good news is Bao will get some more business for his company if our school decides to buy lots of shirts to sell.

So I am happy tonight about all of this. I am happy that I am doing something that I can do to help. And I am very happy that when I tell other people about genocide, they care too.

And then they do the thing that they can do.

CHAPTER 22

DEAR JOURNAL,

Mr. Dr. Steinberg is not dead!
He is still alive, and tomorrow or Friday he will come back
to our class. I know that he will do this because Mr. Dr. Jok told
our class today. He told us that Mr. Steinberg has been out of
town on some business and that he would be in our class again
in the next day or two. So this means that I will see my teacher
on Thursday or Friday.

I am very happy about this good news and I am happy that
my teacher is not dead. Now I am hoping that his kitten is okay,
too. Because if you leave little cats alone without food and water,
they will die. I hope my teacher left enough food and water for
his cat while he was out of town or that maybe he asked somebody to give it some attention. Kittens like attention.

Okay, let me tell you some more things about genocide. I will
tell you about some stuff that is getting done to deal with race
killing after it has happened.

I told you that no real fairness after the genocide in Armenia ever happened. I think some trials sort of happened even
though the guilty people were not there. So nothing major really
happened.

A special tribunal for Cambodia is supposed to have trials
soon. Some top Khmer Rouge leaders will have to answer for
the awful things that happened in Cambodia. But since thirty
years have passed since this genocide happened, a lot of them
are dead. Pol Pot is definitely dead.

So is the Serbian and Yugoslavian president, Slobodan
Milosevic. He died of a heart attack in the War Criminal Prison

in the Hague (the Hague is pretty much the business capital of the Netherlands). When he died, Milosevic was in the middle of his trial that was being done by the International Criminal Tribunal for the Former Yugoslavia (ICTY). The ICTY was set up by the UN to deal with leaders who helped with the genocide in Bosnia-Herzegovina. But Slobodan died in 2006 before a final decision about him got made.

That man Radovan Karadzic is still waiting for his trial. He had run away and hidden for many years. But he got found this past summer and now he is in jail. Ratko Mladic is still a fugitive. A *fugitive* is a person who is running away to escape something. I guess Mladic is running to escape his consequences.

I also told you about some of the justice happening in Rwanda because of the tribunal that the UN set up (called the International Criminal Tribunal for Rwanda). Some trials have happened and some people have been convicted (I already told you about Theoneste Bagosora and Jean-Paul Akayesu, but there are more). Also, there are those gacaca courts that let the local judges help make some fairness. And there is still more to come in the future, Mr. Dr. Jok says.

After the Holocaust, those Nuremberg Trials happened. These trials got some of those men who murdered so many Jewish people (and other people, too) to have to answer for their evil crimes.

And, of course, the Genocide Convention got written.

But nothing really happened about southern Sudan, and there were more than two million people who died. There was no tribunal for the killings that happened there.

Darfur is different, though. This past summer, on July 14th, a lawyer named Luis Moreno-Ocampo filed some charges against Omar al-Bashir. He said that Omar had committed war crimes, crimes against humanity and genocide against the people of Darfur.

Let me tell you about Luis Moreno-Ocampo because he is not just a normal person. He is the Prosecutor for this big court in the Netherlands called the International Criminal Court. A *prosecutor* is a kind of lawyer who brings a charge or charges against a person or a group. He or she does this after getting some information together that shows that the person or group should have to answer for something wrong that was done. The wrong things that were done are the *charges* that get made against the person or the group. Luis Moreno-Ocampo is the Prosecutor who does this at the International Criminal Court. Let me tell you about this special court. *The International Criminal Court* (a.k.a. ICC, for short) is this court that got set up in July of 2002 to deal with genocide, crimes against humanity and war crimes. I think like 108 out of the 192 member states of the UN are part of the ICC.

No countries are forced to be part of the ICC. They get to choose if they want to be part of this court by deciding whether or not to sign and agree to the treaty that made up the court in the first place. This treaty that made up the ICC is called the *Rome Statute* because the things that set up the court got agreed on in Rome in 1998. The reason the ICC got created is to be an independent, permanent court that deals with punishing people who commit genocide and other international crimes that hurt people and groups of people.

The ICC takes genocide and behaviors like genocide very, very seriously and I think that this is a good idea. **And it makes sure that people who would not have to face consequences for genocide in their own countries still have to face charges by the ICC. This is true even if their country has not decided to join by signing that Rome Statute.**

But anyway, in 2005, the UN Security Council asked Mr. Moreno-Ocampo to check into the horribleness of what was happening in Darfur. Lots of research about what was going on in Darfur had already been done. Also, a lot of people who cared about the killings in southern Sudan were using their voices to say, "No. The situation in Darfur cannot be like the terrible situation that killed so many people in southern Sudan."

These caring people who stick up for other mistreated people are called *advocates* or *activists*. I think I told you something about them earlier. But I forgot to tell you what they are sometimes called.

Anyway, these advocates or activists are often witnesses who have been to—or even lived in—places where a genocide is happening. Lots of times, they have seen the terrible things being done to people and their lands. But sometimes they have not been to these places that are suffering. They have just decided that they will care and be doers.

And they say to their governments and to special groups that can make changes, "No more. Enough is enough and we have to interrupt the wrong things that are happening to people. We need to work for change."

So with all the research that had been done, plus the large group of activists saying, "no more genocide," Darfur did not get ignored liked southern Sudan had for a long time.

But anyway, Mr. Moreno-Ocampo did his investigating and did some reports to the UN Security Council about what he found. In 2007, the judges of the ICC put out arrest warrants for two Sudanese government leaders, and then this past July, Mr. Moreno-Ocampo filed that bunch of stuff I told you about against Omar al-Bashir. Mr. Dr. Jok says he thinks that the ICC judges will be issuing a warrant for Omar's arrest, too.

I bet that Mr. Dr. Jok is right. And I bet that Omar al-Bashir will act even more violent if that ICC makes an arrest warrant for him. Mr. Jok said that right now, millions of people in Darfur are depending on humanitarian groups for food and water and medicine. He said that if this arrest warrant gets made, Omar and his NCP leaders will probably do more things that will make the people of Darfur suffer even more. He will probably make a lot of aid groups get out of Darfur and this will cause tons more people to die. And he might even get all of that fighting going again and get the Janjaweed to do more killings.

Hey, do you know what I wish? **I wish that there could be some happy endings to genocides.** I wish that there were some things that could make the horrible stuff that happens during a genocide all better.

But this is probably a dumb thought because there can be no way that destroying races of people could ever be okay. Maybe the closest thing to a happy ending would be that leaders around the world learn from the horribleness of what has happened. And then maybe they all say to themselves and to places where genocide is happening, "No more genocide. Never again." And they really mean it.

I told Mr. Dr. Jok about this idea of a happy ending and he said that it was good and strong. He said that leaders around the world need to have this attitude of being strong about race killing. He said that when leaders decide that enough is enough about genocide, and that they will not let it continue to happen, they would be showing what is called political will. *Political will* (when we are talking about genocide) just means that governments decide that they will not stand for genocides to happen anymore. They will do what they have to do to make them stop. They will also work to prevent them in the first place.

Mr. Dr. Jok says that there is not enough political will among our world leaders when it comes to genocide.

Okay, my hand is tired of writing, plus I hear Liliana and some of her friends buying pizza at the door. So this is a perfect time for me to have a break because I know that my sister will give me pizza without me even asking. I know this because she has been extra nice to me lately.

I will be back soon to write about a few more things.

✳ ✳ ✳

I am back now and I was right. I got to have three pieces of pepperoni pizza and one piece of hamburger pizza that had cheese-filled crust. Plus, I got to have all the root beer I could drink and now my belly hurts.

But I will write anyway.

So before we left our class, our substitute teacher asked us what we thought peace is.

Rusty White said that peace meant that you do not fight with your brother or with your classmates on the playground. Rachel Ling said that peace meant that the American government would stop telling the Chinese government what to do. Rachel and her parents are from Beijing and her father does something in Washington that has to do with the Chinese government.

Mr. Dr. Jok said that these were interesting ideas. He said to Rachel that he did not think that the American government was trying to tell the Chinese government what to do. He said that each of us has a way of looking at the world. All of us have ways that we see our governments and our families and our beliefs.

He said that these ways that we see these things are all formed. They are formed by where we live and who we grow up around and what we are taught about other people and places in the world. **And our teacher said that since there are close to**

seven billion people on our planet, there are a lot of different ways that people see the world!

He said that even though we might see something one way, somebody else who has lived in another place and has been taught different ideas might see the same thing or situation in a completely different way.

Mr. Dr. Jok said that this is why working for peace is so important. He told Rusty—and all of us—that peace is not just not fighting with our brothers or with people on the playground.

Peace is not just having no wars or fighting or genocides.

Real peace is more like having understandings between people and countries—and these understandings lead to safe communities where people are treated fairly no matter what they believe or what color their skin is or what language they speak.

Peace is not all about just being quiet and not hurting or killing. It is about working things out in a way where people from everywhere, who all see the world very differently, all get a chance to be treated with respect. This respect gets shown in the fair and good treatment of others.

This does not mean that all of these countries and people will not disagree. Because they will. But when these very different people disagree, choosing peace would mean that they work hard to mind their manners and not yell or shout or threaten like bullies on a playground. Instead, they spend their energies trying to find solutions to how they can all get along best.

Because like Mr. Dr. Jok said, everybody on this planet is a person. **And a person is a human being before he or she is anything else.** Before I am an Hispanic boy, and before Maker is an African boy, we are both people. He speaks a language that I do not understand with his parents and I speak some Spanish. But our languages are not the most important thing about us. The most important thing about us is not the different colors of our skin or where we came from.

The most important thing about us is that we are people on Earth who are living at the same time and trying to do the things that we need to do to live.

My teacher said that because we have this very big sameness in common, we have much that we can work together on.

And we can—if we choose to—do it peacefully and with great respect.

I liked all of these ideas about peace and I think that Mr. Dr. Jok has learned a lot of very good things from his years of studying to be an expert. Maybe I will be a peace expert if I do not write books that have dragons in them so I can make money to help some people who are having hard times.

I will have to see.

But the last thing Mr. Dr. Jok said was really kind of funny. I do not mean funny in a laughing kind of way. I mean funny in a weird way.

He said that when we disagree with people or have times when we might not like something about a person, we need to think about how they are a person just like we are. Then we need to remember something called the ethic of reciprocity.

The *ethic of reciprocity* is mostly a big way of saying that we should treat other people the way that we want to be treated.

I think that this is funny because Papa says this all of the time and he is not talking about genocides or peace between people and governments. He is just minding his business and being the kind of good to people that I guess he hopes that they would be to him. He says this is called the *golden rule*.

Rules do not have colors so I do not know why the golden rule—which is the same as the ethic of reciprocity—would be the color of gold.

Anyway, Mr. Dr. Jok said that this ethic of reciprocity was something that could be understood by cultures all around the world. He said that more than twenty world religions or philosophies have their own golden rule as part of its teachings. These teachings pretty much say the same thing about how to treat people: People are supposed to treat other people the same way that they would like to be treated.

So this means that if there are people who are not part of the same race or religion or culture as the race or religion or culture that we are part of, it is our responsibility to treat them with the respect and kindness that we like to get. And if we disagree with these people in other cultures or religions or whatever, we are responsible for paying attention to the truth that they are people. And this means that instead of having prejudice or mistreating them because they think or act differently than we do, we are responsible for not throwing fits or picking fights or doing stuff that hurts them.

And countries with different leaders can use this idea to help them figure out ways to solve their problems, too. I mean, we do not have to have wars between countries. We do not have to have races and cultures fighting each other. Wars and fights could stop.

Genocide could end.

The last thing that I will say about this idea is that it would only work well if everybody really believed it and tried to make it work. That ethic is a really smart and cool thing that could help people and governments work out stuff. But like Lili always says, you cannot force people to do anything.

Still, I wish that everyone would think about the golden rule in their culture and take it seriously. Maybe if we all did this, there would be no more genocides.

And if there were no more genocides—I mean ever again—that could be the happiest ending of all.

CHAPTER 23

DECEMBER 18, 2008

DEAR JOURNAL,

The best news ever: My teacher was back today!!!!!!! He is definitely not dead, and guess what? He had a bunch of secrets we did not know about him. He really did.

Mr. Dr. Steinberg is even more crafty than a mole and cooler than a ninja, I think. Except that he does not have a stealthy ninja body. He has a body that is a little like those Santa Clauses that you see in toy store magazines around Christmastime. He looks kind of soft all over and he has a belly that is round but not too big. And his hair would be rock star hair if it was not mostly gray and if he did not have a moustache and beard that matched it.

But here is why my teacher is so crafty and cool:

Mr. Dr. Steinberg was in Africa!

He was in some secret place doing some meetings to help get some peace in Darfur. I think he was in the capital of southern Sudan (which is Juba) meeting with some of those groups of people in Darfur that all have different ideas. Then I think that he met with some of the humanitarian aid group leaders and some other people he did not really tell us about.

My teacher is so completely awesome!

Also, we learned some other stuff about him because Mr. Tate and Mr. Dr. Jok both came to our classroom to tell us the truth about my very cool-stealthy-awesome teacher. This is how it happened:

Like usual, I went into my social studies class where Mr. Dr. Jok was writing a million things to review on the board. On one board he had written these two things:

139

Some Causes of Genocide:
Conflicts between races and cultures
Prejudices about race or culture
Extreme poverty
Conflicts about religion
Conflicts about natural resources
Changes in ecosystems
Impunity

Some Things You Can Do to
Help End Genocide (with Your Parents' Help):
Learn all that you can about genocide—and also about peace-making
Support groups working to end genocide
Support groups that are working to make and build peace in areas where there is conflict
Support humanitarian aid groups that are helping genocide victims
Write to/e-mail/call/visit your leaders in Congress
Call and write the White House
Help get your places of worship involved
Make a special event (like a play or a book fair or maybe a picnic or a pizza party). Tell about genocide at the event and then donate the money from the event to groups helping end genocide.
Create student groups that teach about genocide and help get people involved

On the other board, our substitute teacher had written out the definition of genocide from the Genocide Convention and a few sentences about Raphael Lemkin. Then he listed all of the genocides that we have been studying.

So we all thought that we would be copying down a million things today, but just as we started writing stuff, Mr. Tate came in with Mr. Dr. Steinberg.

For a minute, nobody said anything. Not even Rusty White. Then we all stood up and clapped. I do not know why we did this because we did it even before we knew about the total awesomeness of our teacher.

But we clapped and clapped for him.

For a long time, Mr. Steinberg just stood there and kind of smiled. He stuck his hands in his pockets and he rocked back and forth on his heels. A couple of times he tugged his beard. Then he asked us to please sit in our seats.

We did what he said and Mr. Dr. Jok started telling us the story of how he knew Mr. Dr. Steinberg. Since I already knew this secret information, I was not surprised that my teacher is also a professor at a very awesome university in D.C. I was not surprised that he is a doctor who is an expert instead of a doctor in a long white coat who does surgeries in hospitals.

But I was very surprised when Mr. Tate said that Mr. Dr. Steinberg had been asked by some people in the United States government to go meet with some groups that are fighting in Darfur. Our principal said that our teacher has done this important work of helping with talks about peace for a long time. He said that besides being a brilliant teacher, Mr. Dr. Steinberg has been working for peace and trying to stop genocides for many years.

But until this year, he had never taught students as young as the fifth graders at Roosevelt Elementary.

We were really lucky, Mr. Tate told us. Because not too many fifth graders get taught units on genocide. Most kids our age do not learn about race killing at all even though our principal said that fifth grade is a fine time for kids to begin understanding how the world really works. It is a perfect time for us to learn how we can become involved in things that help make life better for others.

After all of these little talks, Mr. Steinberg said some nice words to us. He said things like he was glad to see us and that he had missed being in our class but he was happy that Dr. Jok could be here. He said that the teaching of genocide to fifth grade students had been a new thing at our school and he was very pleased to have had this chance to teach us.

He also said that his kitten was doing fine. He told us this because Ahmed Naghavi asked if his cat was still alive even though Mr. Steinberg had been in Africa for a while.

Then our teacher asked us if we had any more questions about all of the stuff that we had learned. After everybody stayed real quiet for a long time, Mr. Steinberg walked over to where the definition from the Genocide Convention was written. Then he said this:

"The word for what we've studied these past few weeks, boys and girls, is genocide." I watched Mr. Steinberg turn from the chalkboard to face our social studies class. He looked sort of strange, like he was sad or something. "And if you want to help end it...if you want peace and protection for all people...you have to get involved and do the thing that you can do."

We were all pretty quiet again. I think that maybe we were thinking about all of the things we had learned these past weeks. Maybe we were all thinking about the millions of people who had been killed and tortured. We might have been thinking about the families of the dead people and how hard it must have been for them.

Maybe we were all thinking that race killing should not happen—not ever again—and that we all needed to find the thing that we could do to help and then do it.

I do not really know what all of us were thinking. But these are some of the things it felt like we might have moving around in our heads. Because we were all very quiet, and the air in our classroom felt hard to breathe.

Then I thought about a question I wanted to ask my teacher after all.

"Mr....Dr. Steinberg," I said, "What made you start paying attention to genocide? I mean, why did you get so interested in teaching people about it?"

My teacher waited a little while before he answered.

"That, Javier, is a question that I have not always answered as honestly as I should have. For a long time, I kept a very big secret to myself. I told my university students that I want genocides to end and that I care very much about peace."

"But isn't that true, Mr. Steinberg?" Rusty White looked very confused. But this is normal. Rusty gets confused almost as much as he gets detention.

"Of course it's true, Rusty. It's just that this is not the complete reason why I have spent much of my life working to help end and prevent such suffering."

"Can you tell the rest?" I asked.

Mr. Steinberg looked at Mr. Tate and then at Mr. Dr. Jok. They both smiled at him.

"Do you remember the first genocide we studied, class?"

"The Holocaust," I said.

"Correct, Javier. We studied the extermination of more than six million Jewish people under the leadership of Adolph Hitler. And one of those people who were killed in one of those extermination camps was my father."

I felt like all of the air got sucked from the classroom. For a minute, I could not breathe at all.

Mr. Steinberg kept explaining and we all stayed as quiet as fat little puppies with full bellies.

"My Jewish father and mother were fortunate for a long time during the Holocaust. They were hidden until 1944 by a wonderful German family that rejected Hitler's terrible plan. Then Adam and Bertha Deutsch were betrayed by their own son, who had joined Hitler's SS. When Bin came home for a short rest before getting new orders, he realized his parents were hiding my parents in their home. So Bin turned his family—and mine—into the hands of the Nazis."

I was wishing that I had not asked my question because I could see that talking about this was not easy for Mr. Steinberg. But he kept on telling us the story.

"So the German soldiers stormed the Deutsch's home and promptly captured everyone there. I've never known for certain what first happened to Adam and Bertha after they were seized, but they wound up at Dachau, which is a concentration camp." Mr. Steinberg stopped for a second. He took a deep breath then started talking again. "My parents, Esther and Jacob, got sent straight to Auschwitz-Birkenau. And to make a long story short, the only one to survive was my mother. She was very young and quite beautiful. She was also expecting a baby. And when she arrived at Auschwitz and was separated from my father, the Nazi soldier who was responsible for getting her to the gas chambers did something else."

"What did he do?" Sophia Mandola blurted out, and even though she had not spoken very loud, it felt like she had screamed.

"Rolf Nagel hid her until he could coordinate her escape back into Denmark."

"Why?" I could hardly believe what I was hearing. "Did he know her?'

"He did, Javier. Rolf had known my mother her whole life. They had lived on the same side of town, had known many of the same people. Mother's big brother, my Uncle Isaac, had actually been quite friendly with Rolf. And while Rolf had become hardened and cruel in many ways, I guess the sight of my pregnant young mother did something to soften him."

"So he let her go." Ahmed almost whispered.

"He not only let her go. He arranged for her safe passage all the way back to Denmark. And three days after she arrived, I was born."

"What happened to your father?" Rachel asked.

"Jacob Steinberg died in the gas chambers of Auschwitz, so I never knew my father. And two weeks after I was born, my mother died."

I guess nobody knew what to say to Mr. Dr. Steinberg. I mean, what do you say to something like this? Maybe our teacher was reading our minds because he kept on talking.

"For a long time, I didn't tell about this part of my life because I didn't want people to feel sorry for me. But I've learned, boys and girls, that this is part of the story of who I am. I'm Eliot Steinberg, son of a Jewish Holocaust victim. I'm also Dr. Steinberg, professor of law and international relations and I'm Mr. Steinberg, social studies teacher to some of the world's best fifth graders. Sometimes I'm a peace messenger—which is called an *envoy*—to places of great conflict and I'm the friend of a group of people so amazing that I think every day about how lucky I am to be part of their lives." Mr. Steinberg cleared his throat two times. "Finally, I'm a follower of who I believe to be the God of this universe and, I hope, a faithful advocate for people who are unable to defend themselves in some of the world's most oppressed nations. I'm almost sixty-five years old and if I had my life to live all over again, I would be doing exactly what I'm doing right now." Mr. Steinberg walked over to his desk. It was covered in papers and stuff, so he scooted things around until he cleared a space on the corner where he always sat. Then he sat down.

"When you walk out of class tomorrow, boys and girls, you'll turn in your journals. You'll be done learning about genocide. Some of you won't learn anymore about genocide for years, and others of you may not learn another thing about race killing."

"But that does not mean that genocide is not still happening." I did not mean to, but the words just came out of my mouth.

Mr. Steinberg got up off of his desk and walked slowly to where I was sitting. He looked at me, dead serious, and for a second, I thought he was mad at me.

"Thank you, Javier," he said quietly. "Thank you for understanding this and for saying it out loud for everyone to hear. Because you're absolutely right. When we're all done with this unit of our studies, the story of genocide will still be continuing. And this brings me to one final point."

My teacher walked back to the front of the classroom and stood near the chalkboard that had the definition of genocide on it.

"Every person's life is a story. What I mean by this is that every person's life is filled with experiences and people and places and ideas that are unique to him or her. And because every day is new and different, every person's story is always growing and changing. But here is something incredible: As different as your story or my story may be, we all have this one thing in common—our lives are meant to join with other human lives. Our stories are intended to connect, and when they do, the stories of the people in our lives become, in some ways, our stories, too."

"You sort of mean that we all belong to each other, don't you?" Ahmed asked.

"Yes, Ahmed. That's a good way of putting it." My teacher shook his head. "Whether it's the stories of people struggling in our own cities or the stories of people across the world living in poverty or war zones or through genocides—the fact that we're human and that they're human makes us in some way responsible for each other."

"But we can't fix everything that's wrong in the world," Rusty practically yelled. "My dad says so."

"Of course we can't," Mr. Steinberg agreed. "There aren't quick, easy answers to ridding our planet of war and disease and poverty and genocide. But just because we can't fix everything doesn't mean that we shouldn't do anything."

"So what are you saying we should do?" Rusty was sort of pouting which was fine with me because it was better than the yelling that he usually does.

"I'm saying that when we learn about the misfortunes of others, we shouldn't look the other way. I'm saying that when we see or hear of injustices, we won't forget that to be human means that we're responsible for doing the thing that we can do to help other humans."

Then Mr. Steinberg picked up a piece of chalk. He wrote these words on the board:

Adeste Fideles

Nobody said anything for a minute. We all got real quiet again.

"Who is that?" Rachel Ling finally asked. "What does she have to do with genocide?"

As the bell rang, our teacher answered. "I hope that she is you and you are her," he called as we got our stuff together and headed for the door. "And if you are, this has more to do with helping end genocide than you can imagine."

So I hurried up and wrote down the name of this person. I decided it was probably some cool girl or woman from South America or something, some girl who does good stuff to stop genocides. Maybe she was even pretty, with hair and eyes that are the color of dark chocolate.

I love dark chocolate, especially when it's all soft and gooey from being in my pocket for too long.

But when I got home and got Lili to help me look it up on her computer, I understood the fuzzy riddle of my teacher.

Adeste Fideles is not a pretty girl who helps with stuff that stops genocides. *Adeste Fideles* is a Latin phrase that means be present, faithful ones.

I had to think hard about this for some minutes. And then I understood exactly what Mr. Steinberg meant when he said that he hoped that she was us and that we were her.

CHAPTER 24

DEAR JOURNAL,

So I am turning you in after class today. This is my last time to write in here which feels sort of weird because I have gotten used to talking to you. Also, I have made a decision. I have decided to leave all of your pages in because every page seems almost like it is bone attached to the skeleton of a very large and complicated creature.

I think this is because genocide is complicated. So many things are attached to it. And so are some of the things that happen when people try to learn or teach or do something about it.

I found out yesterday that my genocide t-shirts will be for sale after the winter holidays. They will look very, very cool and I am happy about this. I am happy that because of Bao and Lili and Mr. Tate and Mr. Dr. Jok—and, I guess, me—the kids at my school, and a bunch of other schools in our district, will have the chance to buy shirts.

I will give away the money that I make from them and this is another thing that I am very glad about.

Mr. Tate and Mr. Steinberg are very pleased about my idea, but I am the one who is glad that I learned about race killing. I am happy that I found a thing that I could do to help.

But there will be other things that I can do, too. I do not know why, but I just know this. There will be more things that I can think up and then help make happen.

I want to do these things.

I *will* do these things.

But right now, I am thinking about this last thing: I am thinking about the first day that I heard the word genocide in my class.

I did not like it.

I still do not like it. I do not like what it means and how it destroys and that it keeps happening.

But there is one thing that I do like about all of this. **I like it that I know about something horrible and that I have decided that I will not do nothing about it.**

I will keep doing the thing that I can do and I will try my best to help others do things that they can do.

And like Lili said today, if everyone decides not to do nothing and we all do something, then maybe anything is possible.

THE END

ACKNOWLEDGEMENTS

I'm indebted to the following for taking this journey with me — and for demonstrating compassion for the world in a million different ways: Lizi and Matthew Bailey; Annetta Box; Shelly and John Berryhill; Melanie and Duane Brooks; Cindy and Tommy Brown; Jeannice Cain; Thomas Campbell; Chris and Joni Cristadoro; Kevin Cristadoro; Diyo Deng and Buttrus Jok; Liliana Escobar-Chaves; Amanda Gentry; Lore and Joe Gentry; Roy Hankins; Kathleen and Jim Kidd; Carol Kleckner; Tim Long; Maker Manyang; Linda and Mark Maxwell; Alicia and John Music; Ryan Musser; Sandra and Rob Perkins; Angela and Josh Plumley; Jessica and David Ray; Maureen and Jim Richardson; Shauna and Peter Swann; Dennis Wessels; Laura Winchell and Jengmer Yat.

I'm grateful for the following books; each was—and is—an invaluable resource: *American Foreign Policy Since World War II* by Steven W. Hook and John Spanier; *A Problem From Hell: America and the Age of Genocide* by Samantha Power; *Blood and Soil* by Ben Kiernan; *Genocide* by Jane Springer and *Not on Our Watch: The Mission to End Genocide in Darfur and Beyond* by Don Cheadle and John Prendergast.

A special thanks to Dr. Gale Stokes for invaluable counsel and input; Betsy Smith for always staying in the story; Ashley and Dustin Sullivan for offering countless ideas (like this book's cover) and even more endless support (like reading through manuscripts, enduring a million "what do you think about this?" questions and so much more it wouldn't fit here); Maddie Lizzy for unbelievable and profound sweetness; Olga Lagounova for matchless artistry and infinite patience; Jennifer South for superior proofing skills and generosity of spirit and Velin Saramov for making all the ideas and words come together.

Finally, thank you, David, for caring about what really matters. Thank you for relentlessly doing the right and beautiful thing, especially when no one is watching. I couldn't be a more awestruck witness—and I couldn't love you more.